Dear -
Hope you enjoy it ,

Let Us Look Elsewhere
and Other Stories

Mona Dash

Mona
10/2/22
London

First published 2021 by Dahlia Books
6 Samphire Close Hamilton
Leicester LE5 1RW
ISBN 9781913624040

Some of the stories in this collection have appeared elsewhere, in a slightly
different form:

The Sense of Skin in *Bristol Short Story Anthology 2019,* Natural Accents in
Leicester Writes Short Story Prize 2018 (Dahlia Books) and *May We Borrow
Your Country* (Linen Press), Watching the Aurora in *The Other*
(StoryMirror), The Boatboy *in Dividing* Lines (Dahlia Books), Fitted Lids in
In the Kitchen (Dahlia Books) and Formations *in The Asian Writer: 10 Years
On* (Dahlia Books).

Printed and bound by Grosvenor Group

A CIP catalogue record for this book is available from The British Library.

CONTENTS

For being another home,
Leena, Kumar, Aniketh and Shraddha

Let Us Look Elsewhere

I imagine you come here with expectations. You want to hear tales of the sari, of the mango, of cow hooves kicking up a dry dust you will want to wipe off with a scented handkerchief. You want to hear of lavender, of turmeric, of jasmine soothing the hot summer evening in a distant tropical country. You expect to be told stories of a certain woman, a certain man, in a certain way. You want to feel, but nothing beyond the ordinary, nothing you cannot stomach along with a thick steak, the knife a tad bloody from the rare meat.

Prepare then to be annoyed. Prepare to shake your heads at the lack of clichés. Prepare to throw away the book even. Prepare to be angry that anyone can write these stories, it is no longer the right of the powerful, the strong, the erudite. Nowadays anyone can take up a pen, a laptop, and float words on the page, dipping into history and geography and creating; what we may not expect, tell a story not told before.

The stories I want to write may be nothing you expect or may be everything you desire. I can write about the place I am from, the shores I have arrived at, the people I met. I can write about the accidents, the tragedies, the way people lost breath when they didn't expect to or were maimed and silenced. The blood which flowed when people attacked others, their homes, their bodies. Inspired by the books on war, I can, for example, write about gas chambers or the site where a nuclear bomb ripped the soil and its heart, or through the eyes of a little child whose parents kissed, and were shot before him.

I can fly across continents and write about modern wars, the one where planes drove into tall, proud towers, the ones which continue as delusional youth wield axes and knives or guns or strapping explosives on, aspire to explode and achieve heavendom, annihilating innocent people. Moved by the video of the civil war and watching neighbours bomb the Stari Most, I can explore strife in faraway countries. I can write about the betrayal and naivety which led to foreign countries ruling my own, but that too has been done; the red and blue flag has been replaced a million times by the tricolor, and evil is often equated with the colour of skin.

There is so much to write. Except that it has been written before, in ways fourscore and one, and I want to write something new, infinitely precious. So let me write some simple tales. Stories told in three days.

Day 1: the world will be made, love will be found, love will be had, and creatures sing, dance, collude, procreate, collate. Trees will grow so tall to never let anyone live without a roof on their heads. Crops will grow healthy and fruits will ripen and burst. Birds will sing timelessly. Lovers will never be jealous, and fathers will never be cruel, and children will never die. Words like harmony, beauty and happiness will take form.

Day 2: there will be more of the same, but snakes will

hatch out of giant eggs, grow, mate and slowly slither into lives and loves. Monstrosities will take concrete form, and not wander nebulously as before. Atrocities will be committed and while there will be villains, heroes will stand tall. Our eyes will glisten over when we see men helping children, women helping older frail men, black, white, and brown singing together. We will remember humanity.

Day 3: the last day. Everything will fall. All the stories I have told before, all the words I have embellished into poetry, into songs, all the tunes I have hummed and taught others. Everything will perish. Whether from fire licking us, or water submerging our lungs, or the moist wet earth softly smothering us in her everlasting hugs. Everything will give way to nothing, to the completeness in a circle.

Will that be enough for you? Will it meet your expectations of a writer; a woman, a man, a criminal, a lover, an individual, a communist, a terrorist, a believer, a mother, a friend, a foreigner, a nationalist, or whoever else might need to take up the mantle of the pen? The scourge of the word for our senses to react? Or will there be more demands from you about the perfect story?

I wish I could write about women who are nourished physically and emotionally and spiritually so in return they can give and give; of men who are so strong, they can protect, be gentle. Not of these wild-eyed bare-breasted hysterical women, caught between worlds, between emotions they do not know they have, and angry helpless men, not knowing, given to lawlessness and destruction. All of them caught between selves, between cities, between the past and the present, and searching. But whatever they find, it doesn't seem enough, as if this is not it, this is not the answer. The answer is somewhere. If we explore further, if we travel somewhere else, outside of ourselves, if we look. Let us then look elsewhere, and somewhere, it will all come together.

But, wait, let me write. Allow me my writing.

The Sense of Skin

I watched Ana sleep, her mouth open, the butterfly tattoo on her shoulder poised to fly. Her skin, lavender soap-scented, paper-dry, dolphin-cold. I spooned her and she continued sleeping.

The morning had been busy, with several animals to do. Foxes, rabbits, minks; tool sharpened, inserted into the skin like a needle, taken off like a sock, skin discarded like clothes. We'd learnt from our fathers and uncles who worked on the farm and came home in the evenings, their breath like ice, to the crackling fire in the living room. They brought back pelt that was slightly damaged and unfit to be sold, so we always had warm rugs, furs on our mothers' and aunts' shoulders. They brought back cold cuts of rabbit to pickle or eat with coarse dark rye bread. Here in Ostrobothnia, the scent of skin was always alive.

At home, in the evening I filleted the fish, scales collecting on the blade, while Ana watched me, lips parted, teeth uneven like small pebbles. Ana loves animals, she's the kind who walks other people's dogs, rehomes straggly cats and lets spiders spin webs in dark corners of the house.

'Do you skin your animals alive?' she asked, her bright green eyes trying to hide her disgust. It wasn't the first time she had questioned, or the first time I'd explained.

'We look after our animals. They die peacefully before we skin. Besides, live animals fight back and can hurt with sharp claws, their fur could get damaged.'

'Over-fed, then slaughtered and skinned. Nice.'

'Have you been talking to the Oikeutta eläimille again?'

'I don't need to talk to animal activists. Don't you think I know? Those Arctic foxes in small cages. You ever seen the fear on their faces?'

'It's not that bad at all,' I was sure she had been talking to someone.

'I went for a walk the other day, over to your cousin's side of the farm. The poor foxes, they don't even howl anymore. Scared to silence. They can smell the scent of dying skin.'

'I can take you for a tour if you want. Please don't walk around like that on your own.' She worried me for an instant, I needed to be careful about what she saw.

∞

I had met Ana in a bar in the town, a friend's friend introduced us. I liked her from the moment I saw her, so slim, graceful, so different from me. We got drunk that evening. Later she told me I was the type she liked. Solid, fit, smiling, and my fingers, she loved my fingers. It'd been three months. I couldn't have enough of her.

But I sensed her restlessness, her doubts, her eyes and mind always asking, searching me. Fur farming was not new to her of course, but she was a teacher and I could see she didn't really like it, unlike other women I knew.

'Is there nothing else you can do for a living? Your brother moved to Stockholm. He's a lawyer isn't he?'

'Worse. An Accountant.'

She laughed.

We ate our dinner outside in the summer evening light, sharing the smorgasbord, Ana chewed the fish delicately, I cut my steak, watched the blood release. When I skinned, I was so skilful that the blood didn't spill. Wine glasses in hand, we watched the night come upon us. I felt like taking her right there but she wanted to put away the plates, brush her teeth. She had such a sense of routine.

I watched her as she slept.

∞

I remembered one night when I lay stroking her arm, the freckles on her paper-skin. She liked that.

'I skinned a seal once, so smooth, so cold. Like you. You won't believe how tight the skin is, stretched firm. When I drew it out, there was a drop of congealed blood, only a globule. And the scent! That sort of flesh, blood-smell...' I said.

She stared at me, got up and left. I thought she was going to the toilet, but she didn't come back for a while. I went to the living area, and found her on the couch, curled up like an Arctic fox, a few days old, soft fur waiting to be skinned.

'Won't you come to bed?' I asked.

'Maybe.'

I sat down next to her. We leaned back on the sofa. I said I wasn't sure why I'd compared the seal's skin to hers, and she shrugged. 'You always have those animals on your mind.

Is that how you see me?' I held her, I said it wasn't at all like that. I don't know when I fell asleep. In the morning, she was gone.

Though she spent most nights with me in my cottage on the border of the farm, she had a studio flat in the centre of town.

What's up? I messaged.

Coming back? I messaged after thirty minutes.

She didn't respond all day. When the moon had climbed half-way up the sky, she came back. We made love like we did whenever she went away; desperately, helpless like weeping animals.

Later I said, 'Animal skinning is all I know. There's nothing else I can do.'

'Study. Get a degree. Who skins animals for a living?'

'Us. Fur farmers. Our family has for generations. You can talk to Uncle Vasa and...'

'I just don't like it... It's not normal, you know?'

She still didn't get that it was normal for me. Even though my father was dead, and my brother had moved away, I worked on the farm with my cousins. We were used to feeling the ice-air as we skinned one fox after the other, used to taking delight in a perfect skinning. Our farm was renowned for high quality pelt for generations. Ana the teacher. She just thought everyone had to be a person of letters.

∞

We would never know who complained. Ana? Someone else? It was so quick; we had no time to react. The officials were suddenly there, all loud voices and staring eyes, demanding inspection. Norway had banned fur farming a few months ago. The world was now looking at Finland, and searches happened frequently. They found the animals skinned alive, their mouths swinging in horror. Foxes five times their weight in the wild. Our animals were taken away in vans, yelping in fear. They gave us a notice to stop operations. We would be allowed to start only after six months, when the officials checked and certified us a safe practice fur farm. It would take months of effort, years of work, to re-establish ourselves. A hundred years of family tradition lost.

Ana stood watching in her red shirt dress. It swung loose around her slim curves.

'It was you, wasn't it? 'You tipped them off.'

She didn't react. Her eyes remained cool green. 'You lied to me! You weren't following procedure.'

'It wasn't us. It was the new apprentices. Cousin Timo hadn't checked,' I said.

'Lies again. You knew.'

'You have ruined everything! Our farm is shut.'

'There's so much more to do. You could go out there, into the world…'

'I will. I will get to this out there,' I said, turning away.

'Feel guilty at least! This is it, finally your chance of repentance,' she shouted, her words loud in the empty farm.

I thought of the skinning, the almost orgasmic delight I felt. Perfection. I would miss it. She left and this time I didn't message her.

Cousin Timo blamed me for bringing Ana to the farm. I retorted it wasn't her, but deep down, I too wondered. I shouted he should have been more careful, instead of adopting hasty methods to make more money. We had never fought before; now we didn't speak for days. The days were dull, the farm silent. I needed a break. Then I heard of some friends backpacking to the Far East; Thailand, Cambodia, Bali, India, countries I had seen on maps in school. Despite what Ana presumed, I would see the world. I would forget her waxy-paper skin, the cold air I had grown up in. I joined them. We travelled for months, into the tropics, into the heat. I fell into a mass of humanity I didn't know existed. I was in India.

∞

I am on a train from the Mumbai in the west and will go down the coast to Kanyakumari. The others are in Goa, but I wanted to see more of this country, to travel all the way to its tip. Everything feels different.

There is a confusing array of options to choose from on the train, 1st A.C. 1st class, 2nd A.C. In order to make my money go far, I ask for a second-class sleeper ticket.

'A berth to yourself, but no air-conditioning,' the man at the counter says, his teeth stained from something he is chewing. Later, I will learn it is paan; betel nuts wrapped in a leaf, bright red watery juices. I don't want the cold, I say. I want my skin to feel, to sweat. I want my skin to feel different from the cold skins I know. The man behind the counter gives that characteristic nod I have been seeing in the country, but can't figure if it's a yes or a no.

'Foreigners prefer air-conditioning,' he says.

'What do they know? I will be fine.'

Indeed, the heat makes my skin sweat. It's not anything I have known. It drips from my armpits and I feel it on my legs, my toes. There is a smell in the air, sweat drying on exposed skin. It envelops me. I wear flip-flops, my pale feet among the many brown feet, dusty like theirs. I observe how their clothes hang loose, folds of which are exposed at times, their legs, skinny, hairy. I am used to the silence, to my swift knife spearing warm skin and turning it cold. Here the people surround me and each other. Their eyes smile, even when they try to trick me and charge me extra or want something from me. They look at me in wonder. They ask to touch my skin; they call me gora. 'White is a blessing, white is a godsend,' they say. I am embarrassed.

Inside the train, I have never seen so many human beings in one space, like the minks in a Danish farm I had visited, in cages much smaller than advised. I sit along with six other men on a berth; I like their sweating skin, in shades of brown, light, dark, darker, like the earth outside, like the volcanic soil in the hills of Ostrobothnia. My own skin is paper-white in comparison, transparent, unlike theirs, deep like the earth. My body wants to be lost in this crowd.

Every time the train pulls up at a station, people enter in hordes. Once, the man opposite me shoves a few men, 'Out, get out.'

'Hey, what's up?' I ask, surprised.

'They are from general class. No ticket. Shouldn't be here, Sahib.'

'You mustn't call me sahib.' They have explained it is a sign of respect. I don't understand why they feel I deserve any.

They offer me their food – packed boxes of paratha and spicy pickle – even though I say I don't want it. I am being careful. I don't want to fall ill. They show me how to eat with my hands. I wonder what Ana would make of my cut-to-the skin nails now turmeric stained. I suck my fingers. When the train stops at a station, I step out and buy puris served with a watery potato curry, and glasses of sweet brown tea for everyone.

On the second day, one of the men who speaks English gives me some news. 'There is a foreigner woman from England, and she is walking through the compartments taking pictures of everyone.'

'From your country. She will meet you.'

'I am from Finland, not England.' My fellow passengers don't seem to know the difference or care.

Two women arrive. The men make space for them, dust the seats. The girl smiles, holds her hand out, 'Kate.' English, nice, sensible. She is bleached white-blond and I can understand why it is interesting for the Indians. They stare at her and a little girl caresses Kate's hair, as if she is a doll.

The other girl, dark like the dusk; her eyes are the night, her body shines with jewellery. Long danglers on the ears; I count five holes along her ear, each with a different coloured stud. A nose ring. Bangles on her wrists. A long necklace swings on her breasts. Anklets on her feet, silver and red. Rings on all her fingers. She wears a loose flowery tunic over baggy trousers. Her feet are wonderfully exposed and there are little rings on her toes. I think of Ana. Ana was bare.

'Erno,' I say.

'Vaani,' and she holds her hand out.

I have never seen anything like her. Shining skin smooth seal-like, warm, as if an Aga has been lit behind that skin.

They study together in London. Kate had always wanted to travel in India and Vaani was only too happy to accompany her. Vaani is from southern India, from the very tip.

'That's where you are going, Kanyakumari,' she explains.

'It's so beautiful here,' Kate says.

I agree. 'Do you like London?' I ask Vaani.

'Yes, of course. And you, you like this?' she moves her slim hands in an arc taking in the compartment, the crowd, the men and their families.

'Yes,' I say even more firmly. For some reason I feel defensive, as if she is mocking them.

'Why are you here? You should be in the first class where Kate and I are. Or at least in one of the air-conditioned carriages,' she continues.

'I like it. What's wrong with it?'

'What's wrong?! Come and visit us and then you will know. It's not like all of India is like this. Dirty, crowded. Squalid.'

'If it's so bad, why have you come to this part of the train?'

'She's the one wanting to take pictures. I am her guide, so she doesn't get into trouble.' Vaani's lips are full, glossy. Her mouth curves as if she is laughing at us.

Kate is looking out of the window, her camera through the bars.

'Foreigners don't travel in these classes,' Vaani repeats firmly. 'Out of curiosity, what do you do?'

'I am an animal skinner.'

'Oh boy.' As if the oh boy isn't incongruous enough, she throws her head back and laughs, louder and louder.

'What's so funny?'

'Do people actually do these kinds of things? No wonder you don't care what class you travel on.'

'Fur farming is our family profession. There's nothing to laugh about.'

'Tradition. How cute.'

Kate wants to photograph the compartment; the set of smiling men, the family with the two little girls, me, Vaani opposite me. We smile and hold our fingers up in V signs.

I talk to them. I find myself describing the sunset over the farm, how the sky changes colour, pink, blue, then lights up orange and red for an hour or more until the sun sets. How everything is so quiet when I wake up, the morning air so fresh, when I walk on the grass, the ice crunching beneath my shoes. I walk to the cages and lead the animals out. They know me, they trust me. My hands are magic; I can soothe skin. 'I don't hurt the animals, I am gentle,' I say. 'Even when I skin them.' They listen to me in rapt attention. I notice Vaani rests her hand on my arm, she isn't laughing anymore.

'Why don't you join us for a drink?' Vaani says. Outside, the sun has moved almost the entire span of the sky and I wait for it to sink suddenly like it does here, unlike the prolonged sunsets in Finland. I agree. I follow them. People, so many people, sitting on haunches, standing on their toes, along the length of the train. Then suddenly things are posher, and everything seems as if cleaned in a car wash. It's very private, their cabin has a door which can be locked. Safe for women, they tell me. The air is fresh and cool. Though it's not as cold, it reminds me of my skinning room.

Kate has some beer in her suitcase, Vaani pulls out a small bottle of Jack Daniels. They giggle as they pour the whisky into a metal water-bottle.

'We aren't meant to drink alcohol in here. Indian Railway rules!' Vaani explains, seeing me stare. 'If the conductor comes in and checks, or the guys who bring in our dinner, they won't know what we are drinking. Get it?'

It reminds me there is so much about this place I didn't know, so many things which are different from home. She is looking at my surprise in amusement.

'Ah I see.' And then I add, 'But are you allowed to drink alcohol anywhere else?'

'What do you know?!' she laughs loudly. She sees my clumsy attempt at humour.

We sit next to each other. We talk. 'I have lived long in cold, clean rooms. This stickiness, the warmth on my skin, I like it, do you understand why?' I search Vaani's eyes for an answer.

'Intriguing. So different,' she says, finally. I can see she is curious; I reach out and let my fingers run on her arm. She laughs and Kate rolls her eyes.

It is past midnight. The bottle is empty. 'Time for bed,' Kate yawns. She plugs in her headphones, puts on an eye mask. She has the lower berth and Vaani hoists herself on the top berth.

'Come,' she says, patting the space next to her. I point at Kate, 'What about her?'

'She sleeps like a babe. Also she won't mind. She knows me!'

I climb up and sit, legs folded, head bent. She switches the main lights off and flicks a reading light.

I look at her, her eyes, her skin, mostly her skin. She removes her top, then the rest.

'You smell good,' I whisper.

'Indian jasmine, don't you know?' She has tattoos, small shapes on her arms, shoulders. I see a seal, glowing black on her left thigh. Unashamedly warm. The berth isn't long enough for me, and she laughs that I must keep my legs bent. She lies flat on me. We learn to inhabit the small space, to make the best of it. Am I hurting her? She smiles no. And when I inspect her, as I do my animals, every crevice, every fold, she doesn't judge me, she doesn't call me animal skinner, instead she laughs, she spreads, she arches, she turns around. Open, trusting. She mouths my name, Erno.

All night, her laughing whispers, her scented skin with unfamiliar smells, all night our connected bodies fall in with the train's gentle trembling. I am meant to go back to Finland. Cousin Timo has said the farm will resume soon. But I find myself agreeing with Vaani, yes, I will visit her in Kanyakumari, yes I will stay longer.

I like her skin.

I let the sweat drown our skin.

Natural Accents

After twenty years of living in a country where the sun rose and set at wildly different times depending on the season, and the clocks were changed to ensure a semblance of light when people woke from deeply dark nights, Renuka decided she must acquire a pukka accent. An English accent.

She had just turned forty. She had the detached house set at a respectful distance from the street, a wide garden with roses and apples, a pond where fish blissfully swam to the splashes of a little boy-statue weeing, hedges bursting red and orange in the autumn, a career in a media company, ISA accounts nicely warming in the bank, the children in private schools, the doting husband who was also successful, Joe Malone candles on side tables, Chanel and J'adore bottles on her dresser, diamonds on a ring, and rubies on gold chokers gleaming silently in a safe under the floorboards.

But that accent.

When she spoke, she sounded from elsewhere, from somewhere beyond this green and pleasant land with its Brexited brass walls, from across the seas, like the 'Lord of the Oceans,' the ships that had departed England's shores for days and returned with cotton, indigo and spices at first, then with people, lives and dignities. That accent from a certain part of the tropics, a large country where the sun rose and set at largely the same time in various seasons, where time was sacred and clocks where never tampered with. And grown in one country, hot, fertile, dusty and transported to another country, cool, green and contained, it couldn't shake off its base tenor.

Once, in Soho, she'd asked a passer-by for directions to a restaurant. The bemused man answered in his sing-song Welsh accent, 'I am an outsider like you, and I am lost as well!'

'But I am a Londoner,' she told him, even as he continued smiling, not comprehending. She knew this city well. She had been drunk, she had ranted, she had celebrated, she had kissed in London's streets and parks. It claimed her, it shaped her.

∞

A couple of years ago, their new nanny Megan asked, 'So did you learn English when you came to England?' Megan was making roast chicken for the kids' dinner. Her glasses steamed over as she opened the oven door and checked the half-cooked bird.

'Well, I always knew English,' Renuka could sense herself sounding defensive. 'Most Indians know English.'

'How do people in India know English?' Megan asked, her face a mask of concentration as she plunged the knife deep into the heart of the bird and attempted to cut off the legs.

'The British were in India for years, don't you know? They ruled for some two hundred years?' She sensed sarcasm tiptoe into her voice.

'Oh yes, yes, of course,' Megan said absently. 'Dinner is on the table! Anita, Arjun!'

Efficient, loving Megan who didn't know anything about the busy gallows hanging men to their death and the Vande Matarams that blazed through India years ago, or the reason the land was split and seared.

That night she told William, and he laughed, 'Why would you not mention you studied English in Oxford?'

'Does that even make a difference? If you don't speak English the way they do, they assume you're a foreigner.'

'Look, we all sound different, why does it matter?' His broad Australian accent, the children's clipped British, her polished Indian. William had been brought up in the outback of Australia, on an immense farm so impossibly remote from any other part of the world. Like her, he too had come to England to study and stayed, his language learning the English ways, but his accent drawling on with its idiosyncrasies. The coral reefs, the open air had shaped his calves, his arms, his jaw; large hearted and wide bodied, he didn't care what people assumed.

∞

Some of Renuka's friends put on accents like a quick smear of lipstick. 'Hellow,' they answered their phones, and in restaurants they spoke to waiters, sharpening the 'ta' in a word to a rubber-band snap but after a while, the feigned accent fell limp. Renuka didn't want an acquired accent that changed with emotion, or days or moods. She didn't want elocution classes where some accent tutor would try to train her tongue for months, commanding it to unlearn what it had learnt as a toddler, her tongue remaining stubborn. It had to be ingrained, flowing in her blood. Not an accent training course, nor a tutor, no, she would try the latest method of accent acquisition. She had read about it in the *Metro*, the *Guardian* even: The Natural Accent shop.

∞

She thought for days, and the plan honed and perfected, she told William. He didn't understand at first.

'It's the only way I can truly belong. It's not just about the colour of skin, the clothes, or the food. They are obsessed with accents in this country, and as long as I speak English with my Indian accent, I am assumed to be a visitor. Always from somewhere else, forever.'

'But I speak this way, and it doesn't matter.'

'That's different.'

'Why's that?' he continued looking at her with his half-smile.

'Well, you tick more boxes than me; white, male, Australian, a higher pecking order, you know,' she laughed.

'You are so harsh!' Then he added, 'If the accent is so important to you, then why not?'

∞

Exclusive, in the heart of London. Choose your own accent and walk out a different person, the website promised. Deep

21

in Spitalfields, a picture of the shop, so much like Harry Potter's wand shop in Diagon alley.

After work, the next day, she trailed along confusing lanes until she found it. Innocuous lettering spelling 'Natural accents' in dark purple on a grey door.

Inside, a tract of light, thanks to the expanse of glass hewn into the old brick ceiling. Maps on the walls; changing geographies, countries floated into view and disappeared; words sprang out of blue lakes and mountain ranges, spelt differently depending on the origin. Realize and realise rose from the USA and U.K., baby, bairn and baby from Scotland, England and Wales.

'Hello, may I help you? I am Jim.' A tall, slight man, younger than what she expected, with wavy hair up to his shoulders. This was the way she wanted to speak, the words clipped neatly at the end. The perfect mix of sharpness with softness, just like the chocolate puddings she made with gooey insides, undefined liquid, solid.

'Hi, I am Renuka. I just want to understand how it all works. The service, I mean.'

'Welcome to Natural Accents. This is Harvey.' A little white robot emerged from a door on the right.

'Hi Renuka,' it said. Its face crumpled as if it was smiling. She smiled back at it, no, at him.

'It's very simple. You choose an accent from our vast library, out-of-box or customised. You decide semi-permanent or permanent. You know, like hair colour?' Jim looked at Renuka's hair for an instant, and she instinctively ran her fingers through her sleek curls, browned and blonde over the original black. 'Then we make a couple of small incisions in your skin. Depending on the accent type, the depth varies. Then we insert one of these.' He walked over to the counter and from a wooden box Renuka hadn't noticed before, pulled out a minute circular object like a watch battery but smaller.

'We call this an accent box; you know like a voice box? We place them sort of here,' he ran his fingers on the sides of his neck.

'Goodness,' she said, before she could stop herself. Her voice was high.

He must have read her fear since he added hastily, 'It's not as bad as it sounds. The incisions are small, tiny. You won't even feel it.'

'Our facilities are in the heart of Harley Street,' he gestured towards some more posters over the counter. 'The very best.'

The shelves behind him were labelled: Main Accents of the U.K: Received Pronunciation, Cockney, Scouse, Georgie, Scottish, Irish, Welsh. Under each there were sub-accents.

'Is that the BBC's English?' she pointed at the Received Pronunciation.

'Ah this one. This will give you the traditional form. I do think they need to make a more popular one out-of-the-box, toss the RP in with a bit of today's London, but that's still on the roadmap.'

'Something like yours?'

'I beg your pardon? Mine has a mild smattering of Irish, don't you think?'

'Oh, I am sorry, I am not too attuned to different kinds of accents,' she said hastily as Jim almost looked affronted.

'That's alright, but listen Brogue, Hooligan, Shamrock – do you hear the tones in these words? I wanted to hold on to some part of my roots, hence the customised accent. Would you want to toss in some customisation? It does make it a little more expensive of course. Err, almost double…'

Her budget was ten thousand pounds. She planned to pay for it with her next performance bonus.

'I think out-of-box is fine.'

'Fair enough, but we need to understand something about your background, and your language preferences and things like that. At the end, we will offer a free recommendation of the accent that suits you most. All you need to do is answer the questions Harvey asks.'

'In we go,' Harvey said, and she followed him into a room at the back.

'Like a changing room,' Jim winked and went ahead to greet the elderly Chinese man who had just walked in.

Once she'd agreed to the terms and conditions and declarations of privacy, Harvey asked her question, after question:

'Where were you born? Where are you from? What is the first language you spoke? What is your mother tongue?

24

What is the primary language you converse in? Which language do you use in written communication? Which language do you think in? Dream in? Make love in? Are you married or in a relationship? Do you have children? What kind of an accent do they have?'

When they were done, Harvey plugged himself to a printer and a report slid out. He handed it to Jim.

'It does recommend RP, but throws in a little of standard Indian and Cockney,' Jim said. 'It's like I said, you can consider adding layers in, just to stay in sync with your roots, have your tongue savour what it knows.'

'You sell Indian accents even?'

'Of course. That's the Indian section.'

'But who wants to have an Indian accent?'

'We get all kinds, and remember they can be temporary, so actors often come here. It's quicker than trying to master an accent for a role.'

'I don't want any mixes. Just out-of-box please.'

'OK this is the best quality. You will not remember the old way you spoke English.'

'Right. That's what I need. A pukka accent.'

It was close to ten thousand pounds for an out-of-box top class perfect accent, with a thirty percent upfront payment. If you changed your mind within the first five days you could revert to your original way of speaking. But once the accent box had firmly seated itself, there was little you could do.

Jim had been right. The procedure was fairly simple. It took a few hours for the accent box to settle in her throat, then it would traverse the entire network of veins and help her form words the way they should be.

At home, she read the dictionary aloud perfectly. She said the children's names but they sounded different.

'Why are you saying Ani-tta like everyone does? Mummy, you used to say Anita in such a soft way,' Anita seemed crestfallen.

'She says Arjan like everyone else as well,' Arjun protested.

'Arjoon,' she tried, but it came out 'Aar-jan.'

'This is the way Mummy will sound now,' William said, a mild worry growing in his eyes. 'Don't worry, it will be fine soon.'

The next night, in bed, after a long kiss, William broke away to say, 'Do you think, they sort of changed the shape of your mouth?'

'Not at all. Why do you say so?'

'Hmm, no, nothing, just felt a bit different.'

'I am the same,' she reached towards him.

'Ah, your incisions. Maybe we shouldn't today.'

He looked away.

'What's wrong?'

'Nothing, just a bit squeamish with the blood and everything.

'You have never been squeamish! And these have almost

26

healed.'

'Almost but you can't take the risk. Goodnight, darling,' he said, turning off the lights.

Her husband had never done this before. She lay in bed, listening to him breathe. She mouthed all their names again. She sounded the same, didn't she?

On the third day she went to work. During a conference call, she didn't have to repeat a single word. People seemed to have developed a high level of comprehension.

The next day her boss asked her to join an executive level meeting with their largest customer. 'We think you will be very effective, you are so articulate. And you have the right knowledge.'

She texted William. Honey, the accent seems to be bringing other benefits!

On the fifth day, she called a friend in India to wish her on her birthday.

Nysha squealed, 'Hey, you sound so posh, so English! Pura angrez ban gayi.'

'Not at all, I am still the same person.'

Fresh giggles from Nysha, 'I feel like I am listening to the BBC. Good yaar, when did you learn to speak like that?'

The sixth day was Saturday, and her morning ritual was to call her parents in Odisha.

'Hello Ma.'

'Renu, is it you? Why are you speaking like this?' her mother asked. 'Do you have a cold?' her father added. She could envision them, seated on the blue-patterned sofa, phone on speaker, eager to listen to her voice, their only child. Their home hadn't changed for the last twenty years, and while they had been over to hers, it was always with some trepidation and curiosity about the Australian son-in-law and the mixed children. One light-eyed and brown-skinned, the other dark-haired and light skinned.

'I am fine, just...'

'But why are you speaking Odia like an Englishwoman?'

She heard her father chuckle at that.

'Ma let me call back. Okay?'

Renuka called Jim.

'How's it going, my lovely? You sound great.'

'Thanks Jim. I am fine, but this has changed a lot of things. I can't say Indian names. I don't sound the same when I speak Odia.'

'Pardon? Odia? What is that?'

'My mother tongue. You never told me it would affect other languages.'

There was silence for a minute. 'You never told me you spoke another Indian language?'

'I am an Indian. Of course I speak another Indian language. In fact, I speak three.'

'Did you tell that to Harvey?'

'I don't think he asked... wait. I think he did ask about my mother tongue. Then what I spoke most in... I said English which is true, but...'

Jim interrupted, 'Hmm, maybe you didn't take the multi-lingual questionnaire. Yes, that must be it. You took the standard one which doesn't branch out into all the sub-sections.'

'Jim! I took the one you set me up on.'

'Why don't you come over and we can see what we can do. It's only been five days.'

'It's the sixth day today.'

Jim whistled. 'Ah, is it? Come over as soon as you can.'

Renuka rushed out of the house. Anita was at a birthday party, and William had taken Arjun to play football. She didn't have to tell them yet.

What is your primary language? Harvey had asked. English. Wasn't that the language she thought in, the one she wrote in, the one she spoke and loved in, even when she lived in India? English, the legacy she had acquired, the language she liked the most. But should that love take away something from her core?

Renuka reached Spitalfields in a rush, ignoring the smell of roast almonds, the soaps, a sensuous fragrance stall that seemed to have mushroomed overnight.

'Jim, what can you do?'

He smiled helplessly, 'Just add overtones of Indian English that may help with the names. And maybe the mother tongue. It may just...'

'May? Just may? Aren't you sure?'

'Look, this hasn't happened before. I did tell you it's the

best quality and would completely change the way you speak.'

'But it was RP, to change my English! That's all I wanted.'

'Please calm down. We'll take full responsibility. Don't worry. Could you try and say a few words in this language, Odia? Have a go at saying my name is Renuka and I live in London.'

The words took time to form.

'Mora na Renuka aau mu London re ruhe.'

It sounded different. It sounded unreal.

She watched Jim pick several of those small, curious boxes from various drawers and look at them earnestly, 'Yeah, sounds like more than a hundred degrees of separation between the two languages, hence such a strong effect. You see, the closer languages sound, the less the effect… Harvey, can you come here and help please? We need to map the degrees mate…' Harvey slid over and Jim continued, 'One of this, two of that, let's see, I could get an Odia accented English, yes… And maybe dilute the RP. It should work. Stay calm, Renuka. But let's just hear you again?'

Renuka whispered, 'Mora na Renuka…,' over and over again. Jim and Harvey joined in, the words as if a chant, slowly changing, filling the air.

Secrets

You like the sound of gravel beneath your feet. Crunch, crunch like Toby's cereal, crispy cornflakes in frothy milk. You are walking up the driveway. The house is set right back, hidden behind trees.

'Is this the right address? You're not confusing them, are you?' Michael asks in his usual manner. He laughs and adds, 'I mean, that would be so you.'

You don't react. Instead you point at the sign and say, 'I'm sure it's this one. Garden cottage.' The sign is hanging askew and he impatiently reaches out and straightens it.

'Doesn't look like anyone's in.' He mutters.

'The agent said she would be here. Toby, now come on, straighten up!' Toby is hanging on your arm and you almost trip on him. The rain has been steady all morning and your heels sink into the squelch. Not practical attire for this weather but since when have you been practical?

Someone steps out from a side door.

'Hello, Mrs Smith? I am Debbie from the agency.' An elegant woman, dressed in a smart black skirt suit, a few wrinkles around her eyes.

'Hi, Debbie! Lovely house,' you say, even though you haven't seen any of it yet.

'The owners are away so I will be taking you around. It's lovely, a bit quirky.'

'Quirky is good,' you smile enthusiastically, the way you

are meant to on house viewings.

'Young man, do you want to go in?' she asks Toby.

Toby lowers his chin down and doesn't look up. He doesn't want to look at new houses even though you have explained that a larger garden would be nice for him. Still, Toby doesn't want a change. Michael wants to invest in a bigger property and rent out the semi-detached you are living in now. And you, well, you want something different. You want rooms to rearrange, to become something more. You want alcoves and nooks. Instead of the smooth neutral walls, you want bumpy recesses. You want to hang threads of garlic and pans from a trellis in a large stone-floored kitchen. You want to bake cakes, stir soups, in a kitchen with warm burnt-orange walls. You want to dream, to morph into someone else.

Debbie opens a door off the living room. 'This corridor leads to the spare bedroom and even a little porch outside! This house is full of secrets, I was told.'

And you can see that. The walls are curved. It's like going up a lighthouse. A narrow window is dug deep and on the wide windowsill, a picture of a little girl with blond curls stares out of its silver frame. It pulls at your throat. Toby is five now. People ask sometimes, trying to be funny even Just the one? Where's your second? They comment good-naturedly. They don't know. The miscarriages over the years – the clots of blood passing out like lumps of strawberry jam – your mind holding on in vain to what your body is bent on discarding. The beating, throbbing hearts suddenly

32

quiet, the living warmth turning cold. For years, you had seen blood everywhere. You'd felt it flowing between your legs when there was none, you saw bloodied sheets when you tried to sleep. Your nightmares were soaking red. The insides of a fig, tendrils of pink bits, made you sick. Until Toby. And then the smiles! The joy of blowing raspberries, the clean baby smell, so much happiness at having him, that you didn't want anything anymore for a while. But now you do. You feel the emptiness in your stomach, never to bear, never to be full and round, walk with those sluggish, heavy pregnant steps, yet you don't dare risk going through that again. Michael is done with seeing you weeping silently, sitting still on the sofa, moping a loss which was never to be. 'No more trying, no more babies,' he had said two years ago. 'We can't do that to ourselves.'

'This is the master bedroom.' A velvet red bedspread is draped on the large bed. An image of John flashes before your eyes, you and John, on a bed.

'And just here, tucked in this corner,' Debbie opens two doors. 'The WC here, and the bath on the left.'

'Hmm, so it isn't all in one bathroom,' Michael says.

'You could break the wall down,' you hear yourself say. You have no idea if this is possible. But this sets them off. They discuss if it is a supporting wall. They discuss when the wall was built, and what it would mean for the structure of the house if the wall was brought down.

'We can ask John,' you say.

John knows these things, gardens, houses, anything solid.

You have known John for years. You have known John-and-Lydia even longer. When Lydia, your best friend from university, moved back from up north and bought a house fifteen minutes away from you, the four of you met often, went out, partied, dined. You wept on Lydia's shoulder after your first miscarriage, a year after Toby. Then Lydia had her cancer diagnosis, and you watched her suffer, get well, falter, suffer, and melt away faster than ice-cream on summer days. She passed away just three days after Toby, all plumpness and smiles, took his first steps.

John was devastated. You baked cakes, brought him wine, tucked him into the duvet. Over the years he recovered, became his solid self, always there to help but still alone. When the dimmer in the living room didn't work, when a wasp's nest appeared in the shed, when the kitchen drawer had to be fixed, he came over and sorted it all for you. And when you lost what wasn't meant to be, the third time, you'd held on to him, soaked his t-shirt wet with your tears, the huge bouquet of lilies he had brought, soft on your face. Sometimes Michael doesn't even know something needs fixing.

Last week, after you'd dropped Toby at school, you bought coffee and almond croissants from Costa and went over to John's. Your laptop screen had developed hairline cracks, and John ordered a replacement screen, and so there you were, at nine in the morning, in your crinkle cream dress, ringing the doorbell. John opened the door, all fresh shower smells, in a crumpled blue tee and his faded ripped jeans.

As he worked in the study, you'd wandered over to the conservatory. A thick rubber plant in the corner, its leaves waxy and spilling over from the pot; orchids in many colours, pink, orange, shiny hybrids forming colours yet unnamed. Other flowers from the tropics growing in the pristine calm of England. Once he had presented you with some potted orchids, but they wilted, and then died. Plants, fish, everything, they just die in your house, as if the air isn't conducive to life.

You'd bent down to a shrub, the white wax petals tight in a cluster and breathed from the flowers. A sweet smell of jasmine. You wanted to fall into the smell, to drown in the flowers, or the rain, or the earth, or anything. You kept your head bowed, you wanted to stay there forever, you wanted to sink, like a stone.

'Leela! I fixed it. Laptop's good as new.' John's footsteps fast and hurried. Then a pause and his voice softer, 'Leela, are you alright?'

You are alright, you are never alright.

You stood up close to him while his eyes, blue and anxious, scanned your face. You were the one who took his hands, the well-worn fingers that know how to fix any loose tile, any bit of wood. He looked at you curiously and when you started kissing, you couldn't remember who had moved first, who had swept away the years past, who had brushed away the memories, the foundation of your relationship. Later, your bodies had found each other in his huge bed, his fingers on your face, and he traced its outline as if he was carving wood, carefully, deftly. And it was much later, only when it was time to pick up Toby that you had left.

'I have died, I will lie here forever,' Toby declares. He has flopped on the red carpet.

'Come on Toby, behave,' Michael says.

You have seen houses all day and this is the last one. Toby has kept himself occupied making up imaginary battles with his Spider-Man and Iron Man figures, but you can see from his movements that he is bored. He can't wait to be home and neither can you. The houses are beginning to blur, and peeping into other people's rooms, looking at their pictures, their furnishings, their lives, is taking its toll.

This house is speaking to you. The small study, the irregular bedrooms, a balcony running across it, you can see yourself here, hiding in its depths, spending mornings looking for secrets, stepping over the uneven pedestal into the kitchen. You step outside into the garden.

Purple clematis blooms over a trellis just like the one in John's garden. You'd once said it was your favourite colour and John had come by the next day with a variety of purple blooms for your garden, iris, clematis, even wisteria. A small pond is dug into the soil. You edge closer, the water is dark, deep… you see a flash of red suddenly. You step back.

'Mummy, Mummy!' Toby is calling. He's followed you outside and is pointing at a set of cherubs near the pond, 'I can see their…. willies…' He can't stop laughing.

'Let's go back in,' you say. You are flustered.

'Why do the owners want to move?' Michael is asking Debbie.

'They are getting on, their daughters, all four of them have flown the nest. A lot has happened... a few stories in this house... my manager was telling me… It's seen many a life…'

'The pond…,' you start.

'Yes, there is a little pond. It's not hard to manage, or you can even have it filled.' Debbie answers before you have framed your question.

'Are you alright?' Michael asks impatiently. He turns to Debbie and tells her firmly, 'We will have a chat and get back to you.' Before she can ask him anything more, he says, 'Let's go home now.'

'Yay!' shouts Toby.

In the car, Michael says, 'It's a good-sized plot but we will need to get a lot of work done. An extension strip the walls and change all those green carpets. Is the house worth the asking price? I will have to work out a comparison tonight and…'

'Green carpets? They were red.'

He stares at you suspiciously. 'Have you been seeing things again? You have been acting stranger than usual all week.' Michael sees everything in black and white. When you got married, and everyone said opposites attract, you had smiled in agreement, but over the years, his sense of ordering everything in neat drawers makes your head hurt.

'Yes, yes, I'm fine. Just confused, the bedspread was red…,' you don't dare bring up the pond.

Michael doesn't question anymore. He thinks things left undiscussed are things sorted. Sunday evening and at home, you will make dinner. You will get Toby into bed, then lie in your bed, until your thoughts drown you, smother you. Michael will watch some TV over a drink and then do a detailed cost benefit comparison of all the houses you have seen. He likes to invest, watch his stocks grow.

Tonight, you toss and turn, you wake a few times in the night. Michael is fast asleep and snoring. The rain is steady, caressing the windows, the rooftops. Your dreams are hazy, making you restless. Memories, thoughts, moments, John, Lydia, Michael, Toby, the house, everything dances in your mind like a kaleidoscope. You don't know when you fall asleep.

Monday dawns as if a different country; sunny and hot. After you drop Toby at school and are driving back, John calls again. You ignore it. Holding you close that day, he'd said how he loves the curve of your arms, the way your nails are irregular. He loves children. He loves Toby. He has so much to give, and so do you. How easy it would be! Move out, move in. But… he loves Lydia still. And you love Lydia. So how could you? you ask yourself. You picture Michael's anger. 'Wasn't Lydia like your sister? You bitch!' You imagine Toby's confusion – divided weekends for the rest of his life, split houses. Then you think of growing old, you and Michael alone. Toby somewhere else with his girlfriend. A vision of a silent house, there's nothing you can talk about, no one to talk to. Michael with his excel sheets, his stocks. You sitting near the pond, alone, secrets submerged.

On impulse, you turn into the lane and drive to the house. You want to see it once more. The owners are away and it's unlikely Debbie would have organised a viewing this early on a Monday.

You walk up the driveway. It's like another world, the trees shield the house from the outside, and the house itself seems sunk in the ground as if wanting to hide.

You walk towards the porch, and round to the pond. You notice a bush full of deep red roses, the blooms heavy, next to the pond, a little bench. You dare yourself to look at it again….and again. Sparkling reddish, the sun catches the water. As you keep looking in, you see it, a mosaic of tiles in the pond, different shades of red. That's all it was. You sit down and look in, now you spot some fish. You can smell jasmine somewhere, just like in John's conservatory. A small shrub of white flowers is at your feet. Almost like waxy clusters of jasmine.

Suddenly your phone rings loudly in the silence. You get it out of your bag. You know who it is. You walk out quickly, your heels crunching into the gravel, your hair flying as you start to run. For now, you know what you must do.

The Boatboy

Dhenkanal, Odisha, India, 1938

The river grew wide at this time of the year, increasing in girth every passing day. Baji liked to sit on the banks and watch her swell.

'She is big, she won't grow anymore,' his mother would say.

'If she remains like this for a few more weeks, the paddy fields will be full,' his father would hope. Together they would dream, a bountiful crop, food the year round but that was when his father was still alive.

When Baji was only six years old his father was claimed by a fever for days, then weeks. The kabiraja concocted a bitter paste to drink with water every night, the village priest visited to drive away the evil spirits. They assured he would be well soon. Instead, his father returned one evening from ferrying the boat and collapsed. Baji reached out to touch him. His fingers recoiled. His father was stiff. He hadn't understood. His mother had started wailing, banging her head on the door of their hut. Within minutes, the villagers arrived. They had to take the body, they said. Someone carried Baji on his shoulders to the masani, the graveyard on the outskirts of the village. It was the duty of the son, however young, to light the pyre. The body laid on wood, some marigold flowers thrown on the coarse sheets,

40

nothing elaborate 'For we are not like the wealthy Raja or his Zamindars,' his mother said.

It had been seven years, yet he couldn't forget the heavy stick he'd been handed and advised to bring down hard on his father's head. 'It breaks the skull and lets the insides burn,' they'd explained. They wiped his tears. They gave him a banana to eat. For years he would remember how his father's hand had suddenly jerked up. They said it happened when the logs of wood burned and dislodged the body, burnt black; as if to say Bye-bye, ta-ta the way he did when he left for work in the morning. Ta-ta, and Baji would wave back until the boat grew smaller and the water was still once more. Ta-ta.

∞

The villagers worshipped Brahmani; calming her anger when she threatened to flood, praying for her waters to fill when there was a drought. The fields spanned their village Bhuban, then all the way up to the village of Ranpur.

Like the other boatmen, Baji's family lived on the banks of the Brahmani. His mother worked in the farmers' houses, grinding the paddy to husk. Baji went to school in the day, and in the afternoons, ferried the boat. The boatboy they called him. The villagers paid his mother with rice and grains. Sometimes he would catch fish; the silvery kokila flashing in the shallow waters which his mother fried with salt, but only for him. 'Never, Baji, never!!' she shouted when he placed one small fish in the mound of rice she was eating. As a widow, she could only eat vegetarian food, cooked with no ginger, garlic or onion; it was as much a sin to offer non-vegetarian food to a widow, as it was for her to eat it, she explained. It seemed the whole world conspired to add to his mother's sorrows, Baji thought.

∞

Once a month, the villagers were called upon to do bethi, work for the king, but with no wages. The palace on the hill, Yatna Mahal had been built through bethi. It had taken ten men five days to hang on the ceiling a decoration of lights and glass. It had come all the way from London, chand-elier they called it.

'But why should we work without wages?' When Baji asked his mother, she would panic, cover his mouth with her small hands, silencing him, 'He's the king, the Raja. We have to serve him.'

Once, the villagers were instructed to cook kheer for the king's palace. Baji and his friend Fagoo watched, eyes popping, the milk from twenty cows, thickened, the rice soft just once to slurp that milky, sweet thickness. They were not allowed a single spoonful.

'But why must we cook for them and part with our food?' he asked.

'So much trouble,' his mother whispered. 'You will get into so much trouble.' She sat him down and explained the laws of the land. Bethi was only of them. There was begari, when they had to carry the luggage of the British officials and Indian kings, free of charge. There was rasad, when they had to deliver goods, free of charge. They could do nothing to change these rules.

His mother wore a widow's white, the aanchal covering her head. Her large eyes shone, tears in them, as always.

'Why are you crying again, Bou?' he asked, at which she sobbed louder.

∞

Baji looked at his reflection in the water, his bare body, the half dhoti, yellowish white, a bit tattered, tied firmly so that it didn't slip off. One day, he would leave Bhubhan, leave Dhenkanal District itself, and work in Cuttack. One day, he would wear a hat and coat, and speak in English. He would be a sahib, just like the Englishman, the Political officer of Orissa, who had come to their school last week.

They had prepared for the visit for months. On the day, the school was swept. The children came in clean clothes, faces scrubbed, hair brushed. They gathered for the assembly. Every child received a ladoo; Baji held the sweet, orange ball in his hand, wanting to save half of it for his mother. His bites were too big perhaps, for very soon nothing was left, except for the taste of sugar and ghee on his tongue.

The sahib was tall, his hair shone. He wore dark glasses, so that the sun didn't burn his eyes. In bilat, England, there was no sun; the moon lived in the sky permanently. In bilat there were no huts, everyone lived in houses, for there were no poor people. It was hard for the sahibs to come and live here, but they did. They were not used to the heat, the dirt roads. 'We have to look after them,' their teacher explained. So the boys did. They fanned the sahib, standing in a circle around the tall wooden chair he sat on. Major Bazelgette, they tried to say his name, the syllables falling of their tongues. 'Majjor Bajjelgette', 'a softer zzz,' the teacher instructed, but try as he might, Baji could only say, 'Bajjelgette.'

∞

Nayantara, one of the village widows, lived with her parents, in the last hut, right where the bank sloped, and the mud was even softer. Sometimes Baji saw her, sitting outside in her white saree, feet draped in the water. Her husband had died a year ago and she had been sent back home by her in-laws. Everyone had gathered, Baji among them, to watch her walk back into her parents' house, face lowered; her parents not happy with the returned guest. A daughter's place was with her husband and in-laws, after all. Everyone was commiserating the parents but no one seemed to notice that Nayantara's eyes were red, mouth misshapen, as if she had cried for hours. When he mentioned this to his mother, she nodded and said things would have been worse if Sati was still in practice.

When Baji thought of Nayantara in flames, the fire burning her body just like it had burnt his father's, he could feel the fire in his nostrils.

Sometimes Fagoo came in the morning, when the sun was still feeble in the sky, and waited with him by the boat. One such day as they dug pebbles out of the mud and flung them into the water, he nudged Baji. A slim body in the water, white saree sticking to her legs, Nayantara was swimming fast, furiously. Baji looked away, but Fagoo stood still and stared.

'Is she alright?' Baji worried. Was she trying to cross the river? Did she need the ferry?

'Ssshh, of course she is fine. She is having her bath. I want to watch her.'

'You shouldn't.'

'Why not? Married at fourteen, widowed at sixteen, barren after two years, isn't that what they say about her?'

He wanted to do something which would silence Fagoo, make him look away from Nayantara's lithe form.

But just then, someone called out, 'Boatman! Hey, boy!'

At the sound of the voice renting the still air, Nayantara disappeared, a flash of white, a flash of brown and gone. She must have swum underwater, but Baji didn't see her resurface, and the three young men were right there, ready to step into his little boat, talking animatedly.

'You are the boatman, not him? Can you row us all across?' one of them asked, looking disbelievingly at Baji. Fagoo was so much bigger than him, but he was fifteen, a year or older than Baji.

'I can. I do this every day,' he said.

Out of all the people he had ferried, there was something

different about these men. Almost as if they stood straighter, their voices louder, none of the whispers he heard from the other villagers. Baji heard the word bethi a few times. He strained to hear better.

They came back the next day. One of them even smiled at Baji as he got off the boat.

Back and forth the river, a few times in the month. Who were they? Where did they go?

'Mohanty will join us, only a matter of time,' one of them said.

'Yes. We need more people like him. He refused to do bethi this month. They did a lathi charge, but he resisted.'

Baji, mustering courage interrupted, 'Can we resist? Can we refuse to do bethi?'

'Boy, what is your name?' the one with the moustache asked. His face was serious.

'Baji Rout.'

'And your father's?'

'He died some years ago.'

'By the king's orders, no doubt!' one of them laughed.

'I am Baishnav. This is Raghu, and Gobinda,' the other man said pointing to himself and then the other two. 'We are sorry about your father. But that is what they do. They make us slave, we die, and they eat... and eat.'

Baji remembered his father, his thin frame standing firm on the boat as he rowed. The vest he wore with three holes, one much larger than the others.

'One day, Baji, it will all change. We will make it change!'

Baishnav's eyes looked ahead, farther than where the river lapped on the other bank.

'Do you go to school?'

Baji nodded.

'Can you run an errand for us?' Rabi asked. 'One of our friends will come to the river bank tomorrow in the evening. Can you pass this note to him? He will come up to you and say hukum. That's the cue.'

They gave him a whole anna and waved at him when they got off. Baji waved, Ta-ta, the coin tight in his fist. Hukum meaning order. Hukum, hukum he practised all the way home.

The next evening, a young man, wearing a khadi dhoti stood at the riverside. Baji knew it had to be one of them even before he said the word. He knew from the gait, from the look. They exchanged smiles.

∞

'We will overthrow the Raja. The British are helping him and encouraging his practices. They will have to leave our country! We will be free.' Baishnav declared.

'But Bajelgette is so good, so kind. He talked to all of us,' Baji said.

The men laughed. 'Good?! They rule us, they are not of us. They need to go. The king needs to go. We, the people need to rule.'

'You will be king?' Baji asked.

'No, not I, Baji! We will rule! You, I, this will be our

country!'

'But how?' Baji asked.

'We have to act together. In this struggle, everyone has a role. Even you, Baji, can help.'

Fire in their eyes, fury in their voices, bodies taut and straight, the wind streaming through their locks.

He told his mother about them, the brave founders of the people's movement, the 'Prajamandal.' The voice of the people against injustice, against the authority of the king.

'The Raja will become a common man and the British will finally leave! We will be free!'

'Ssshh, Baji,' his mother said.

'Hukum, Hukum,' he laughed.

∞

Baji waited. The messages now arrived in the stillness of the night. The soft, barely there footfalls, the young man who held his hand out and passed a note, greenish paper folded tightly, then disappeared as quickly as he had arrived, from somewhere between the huts and trees. The next day, Baji would hand the note to a teacher in the school, no words spoken, taking care not to be seen, telling no one else.

The men praised him, patted him on the back. Sometimes they gave him two annas. 'You are one of us,' they smiled as the boat bobbed gently on the river. Someday it will all change; the promise was strong. India will belong to us, the people. The fire of freedom.

He felt like anything was possible. He felt like the time

he had swum the river's breadth, cutting across the water faster than anyone else, then looking up, had seen Nayantara watching him. Surely her eyes were on him, surely she had smiled at him.

The next time his mother cooked fish, he counted four of the kokila, and clutching them in his closed fist, ran to the last hut. Nayantara was sitting outside the doorway, face blank, looking out towards the river. He held out in his hand, streaked turmeric, the crispy fried fish. She stared without a word, then looked back inside the hut hastily. For an instant he thought she would call out to someone, and they would come charging out. But in a quick motion, hardly touching his fingers, she grabbed them all and ran towards the riverbank. He followed, watching her hand move quickly to her mouth, her teeth chomping. She smiled at him, only at him.

He rushed back to his hut, heart pounding.

∞

Baji stood on the banks, one night, the note in his hands, waiting. The river was swelling, the boat bobbled unsteadily. An unusually heavy rain for October. His mother would be so upset if she knew he was here standing in the dark, the moon hidden, drops dripping from his hair. But she slept deeply, the sleep of the tired.

Then he heard some footsteps, unmeasured, like some clumsy beast dashing through the forest.

Baji saw them, the police, their hats, their guns. Their

brown uniforms, brown faces. Two hundred and twenty, the numbers would be written in history, rightly or wrongly, for posterity. He stood stolidly, feet wet, his heart knowing something would happen.

'Boy, take us across,' the first policeman said.

'We are looking for some men. We have burnt Ranpur down. Now it is the turn of Bhuban,' another shouted. There was a surge of laughter in the group.

The rampage was evident. Some looked dishevelled, blood spattered on their uniforms. They laughed and spoke in the language of the big city of Calcutta, Bengali. Baji had heard it once in school. It was said the sahibs had recreated London in Calcutta. Raja Singhdeo had been to Calcutta, even to London. The palace had photographs of the Raja in a carriage in London.

One day it would all change. One day. Even Baji could help.

'The Brahmani is full today. She doesn't want anyone to cross her,' he said, forcing his voice to sound as loud as possible.

'Don't give us advice. Ferry us now. We have to go to the other side.'

'I will not.'

There was laughter. 'Do you know how to ferry a boat?'

'I do, but the boat is not for you.'

The policemen shouted again, 'Get the boat out for us.'

Baji refused. One of the policemen came closer and shoved the bayonet against him. It struck hard on his shoulder. Another hit Baji's knee. He buckled, falling into the soft river mud, letting the note sink so it could never be found. Then, quickly scrambling up said, 'You can cross the river but over my dead body.'

He had to stop them.

'Cross the river we will! Do you know Baishnav Patnaik and Raghunath Mohanty? Where are they?'

Baji knew Raghu bhai's blue kurta well, how he flicked his hair when he spoke. He knew how Baishnav bhai could swim across the river in ten minutes. He knew they had to live to lead India to the promised victory.

'No, I don't.'

The police looked at the rising waters. 'If they have jumped in, they will have died by now.'

Then again, 'Ferry us or tell us where they are!'

When he refused yet again, another policeman hit him. Right on the head, he felt the pain enter and descend into his body, weakening it. He fell, but this time the police restrained him, their feet on his chest, not letting him rise.

'Hukum! Run! Run! Flee. They are here, looking for you!' he shouted. A high, young boy voice over the rivers, a warning to whoever understood, whoever could hear.

'Prajamandala ra hukum nahin. I have no orders from the Prajamandala to ferry you. They are the only ones I obey.'

The police laughed louder. Baji wondered, how many feet stood above him, how many guns were pointed at him? He would never know. The shots rang out, again and again.

∞

51

With all the commotion, the villagers would gather and watch some of the policemen row themselves away in the boat, firing randomly as they went, killing three more men. The rest would storm through the village. Baji's mother would cry all night, her son's head, still, in her lap. Baishnav, would arrive, anger storming his eyes and cradle Baji's thin, still body. Gobinda, Raghunath, Ananta and many others would summon the villages and together they would take Baji's and the other dead bodies to Cuttack. People would leave their homes and join the procession, the masses swelling in broad daylight. A hero's farewell. They would sing when his pyre was lit, when the fire rose high in the skies. 'Nuhen bandhu, nuhen, eha chita, e desha timira tale e alibha mukati salita. Friends, this is not a pyre. This is the fire of freedom.'

Nayantara would sit alone on the bank for nights.

∞

Some months later, Major Bazelgette would be killed by an angry group of protesting villagers. Nine years later, the villagers would be free, both from the King and the British.

India would achieve independence in 1947 but split into two, a scar remembered forever.

As for the boatboy, like so many others, he would barely be remembered, rarely written about, the youngest martyr of India.

Watching the Aurora

The water squelched as I sat on the bench. Steam turning into water, then flowing and accumulating in the crevices of the shiny blue tiles. Trapped under my white swimsuit, when I shifted a little, it squelched louder. I was the only one in the steam room. Dim-steam enveloped, I sat back and stretched my legs. The heat rose, calmed my face, stroked my body. I loved the saunas, steam rooms, hot pools dotted all over Iceland.

In the sauna, the smell of wood. The pine pail with its wooden ladle sat in a corner. I liked to scoop the water, pour it on the coal and watch it smoulder. The wooden walls hazy in the smoke, the smoke on the wood, like a morning fog. In the steam room, the wetness. The – I can't see it but can feel it – kind of wetness. Now I slipped the straps off my shoulders, right down, to feel the warmth on my bare skin. I could feel the sweat drops forming on my chest, on my back. I would have stepped out of the swimsuit if I could but the rules were strict – steam room with swimsuits, sauna without.

The door opened and a man entered, two shadowy children shapes behind him. I pulled the straps up quickly. What was he thinking, wasn't there a rule that children below six weren't meant to be in a steam room? The boy looked four or five at the most. I wondered if I should say something, but I wasn't on duty. I was just another guest now. The children squirmed as they sat down. The girl squelched, the dad squelched, the boy laughed.

'Daddy, you farted!'

'It's just the water,' the dad said.

'It's too hot in here. I want to get out,' the little boy stamped his feet.

'I told you it would be but you insisted on coming in.'

'It's not hot. Harry is a baby,' the girl said.

'Harry, please can you sit down for five minutes,' the dad said.

The children sat still on either side of him. They looked at their feet. They inspected their hands. The dampness grew around their faces and they shut their eyes, smarting. I leaned back, shut my eyes. The vapour made me feel sexier. It made me want him even more. Mark. It made me think of his hands, which would always start by stroking my back. I would let him, and then twist the ring off. Sometimes it was tight on his finger.

'It isn't coming off. Can't you let it be?'

I wouldn't, sometimes I let it rub sharp on his skin as I twisted and turned. 'At least be ring free,' I would say. Free of the bond, if not of guilt. He would smile. Once, we could only take it off after I forced him to soap his hands thoroughly, and the bubbles allowed it to slip it off smooth.

The moisture swirled around me, beads condensing. I watched the blood drop. Perfect red globules from my left arm, one splat on the dampness, the second fell close to it, shapeless immediately. I had to leave. The children didn't notice, whining as they were. If it is this uncomfortable, why don't you just leave? I wanted to say.

It was a small cut, swiftly done, with the red handled knife I cut cucumber with. I sliced cucumber into circles, stacked them on the middle of the plate, and ate them one by one, sucking the soft middle. That little knife had made a deep cut it seemed.

I hoped the father and kids wouldn't notice anything; else I would get into trouble. I wasn't supposed to use the steam or sauna when I had open cuts.

The spots of blood would slowly enlarge into the condensed steam and lose colour. They wouldn't notice, I was sure.

∞

Mark had set the rules, starkly clear. I wasn't meant to make any kind of contact, call, text, WhatsApp, unless he initiated it. I had to be reactive since you never knew when someone else had his phone. One of his three boys. That little buck toothed one, or the one with the long black hair, or the one like him, with the thick eyelashes and dimples. Or his wife, that long-haired brunette. I had seen them all. Why couldn't he keep his phone away from them? But apparently his phone, like his self, became their property the minute he entered through the door.

So he got himself a pre-paid number. Even then, I had to be careful. I could WhatsApp when I wanted but not expect a reply. I would have to wait for the sun to stake its claim on the skies, though I might have spent all night messaging. I wasn't allowed to call, and even if I did, I couldn't expect he would answer as he had the phone on silent. Sometimes I kept his old iPhone back with me. I would send messages to him and watch them appear, then read them and write back to myself. He would smile when he read them to me, said that's exactly how he would have responded.

Not that Mark was my first love but certainly he was the most special. Maybe it was the age, the experience? Or just the words he would charm me with, when he could. I worked in Costa and that's where I saw him, every Saturday from about ten in the morning – casual in his ripped jeans, a t-shirt, hair floppy on his forehead, eyes distant – on the brown sofa in the corner, working on his laptop, coffee long over. Once, I brought him another, and he smiled without asking why. He paid for the extra of course.

'Hi, are you a writer?' I asked the fourth time I met him.

'Hey! Why do you ask?'

'Well, you come here every Saturday, you have your head down and are typing continuously… sometimes you look around but without really seeing anyone.'

He smiled like I had spoken profound words. 'Not really a writer. I am a banker in the week but a writer on the weekend.'

I told him I was impressed. I noticed his ring but didn't mention it. I imagined his life. The terraced house in Chiswick set away from the high street, but not too far from it. The bay windows, the cosy living room, the wife, the children, the stained-glass table lamps, the chaise lounge, the intimate dinners with friends, the dog – 'No, we don't have a dog,' – he'd said later.

We exchanged numbers after a couple more weekends. Funny to think how easily you can bare when the medium isn't voice. It wasn't long before we were asking each other blush-inducing questions; the first fuck, the best positions, the pet hates and received frank answers. I couldn't use my phone at work so I would take toilet breaks and send him messages. I stayed home in the evenings and wrote to him.

It wasn't long afterwards, maybe a week or so of messaging, when he turned up, outside the front door. I used to share my place but the flat mate left, and I was stuck paying a higher rent than I could afford. Now I was living in a cupboard at the top of a two-storey house. Even then, he was gracious. He complimented me on the couch, an overused soft cream sofa, into which we both sank. The narrow bed we managed to squash ourselves into. He only had two hours, but we made the best of it. After that day, he spent less and less time in the café. I changed my shifts to Sunday. Saturdays were our days, sometimes he wrote a little while I slept. I liked to nap knowing he would be there when I woke.

He assumed I was a writer as well. I had to admit, I wasn't one for words. I liked to dance, I loved music. I dabbled with colours. I used to paint as a child but hadn't in a while.

'Maybe you should try. I can sense you have an artist's soul,' he said. We sat on my little bed, sipping the wine he had brought for me, our toes interlaced.

I had my back tattooed that weekend. Monet's lilies trailed down to the base of my spine, and Mark followed them with his fingers now it had healed.

∞

One Saturday, his wife went to the café, and not finding him there, called. His face froze when he answered his mobile and realised where she was.

'I couldn't write at all today, darling, I took a walk. I will be back soon.'

Later, he said she didn't encourage his writing. She couldn't understand why a grown man would hunch over a laptop, instead of playing golf, or taking the kids to football like his mates did. She had once deleted an entire folder off the family computer in anger. He never wrote at home now, though she knew he was writing at least she didn't have to see him engaged in this senseless pursuit.

That day, he'd left a bit earlier, since they were going out for dinner to the local Italian. I took myself out as well. I sat in the corner table by the door, and watched them come in, the children trooping after the parents, arguing, at times laughing. I watched them as they ordered, as he tasted the wine, swirling the redness expertly, nodding his head in acceptance. We didn't talk to each other but he acknowledged me, the faintest of smiles, a special look only for me.

He messaged late at night that he had been distracted all

evening. He'd wanted to come over to me, sitting in my light-gold off-shoulder dress, with my rose-gold flower pendant shining on my clavicle. He noticed everything about me. So I did it a few more times. I went to the park for a run at the same time as them. I was in the swimming pool in the leisure centre, sharing the same pool. I shopped in Waitrose on the weekends like they did.

That's when he said I must stop stalking him.

'Stalking? I am not stalking you! I thought you liked seeing me around.'

'I do like to see you but on my time. Not when I have my family with me.'

I said I would stop.

'I am sorry. Do you know how hard it is?' he smiled helplessly.

But he didn't come to the café on Saturday. Neither on Sunday. He didn't answer my WhatsApp. On Sunday evening I went to his house. I stood on the opposite side of the road, just behind the large English plane tree, willing him to show up. I stood in the darkness for more than an hour. Eventually the lights were switched on in the kitchen and he stood there, at the sink, washing up. I saw him turn and call out to someone. I saw her come in, remove something from the fridge and come up to him. They looked at each other, she leaned towards him. I had a vision of horror that he would slip her jeans off, and take her suddenly, on those polished granite tops. But she was only reaching out for something.

Then he noticed me standing there. I had left the refuge of the tree and was on the sidewalk, exposed. I saw the shock on his face, the furtive look around. He left the kitchen. Minutes later he was outside looking over his shoulder at the house.

'What are you playing at?' the anger in him hissed. I could see it like the smoke from the instant noodles we had shared, hungry from lovemaking. 'I haven't had this rubbish since uni,' he had laughed. 'You are such a child!' He had kissed me again, the noodles dripping into my mouth.

I tried to explain but he looked a different man. I grabbed his hand. And that made him angrier. His face close to my ear, he said, 'Go home!'

I left. All night I cried, waited for his text.

I had moved back to London from Rome, after my boyfriend and I broke up. Giovanni said he needed to fly but I needed a cage. I wanted to imprison him apparently. He moved out of the flat. He changed his number and blocked me from his social media. That's when I knew I had to leave. I came back to England where my parents lived. Where else could I get back on my feet, perhaps study further, get a job? When I had first seen Mark in the café, I had no plans. I had just enrolled for an evening course in graphic design. Life was waiting for me.

Mark told me a story about the girl who lived in the Aurora. The girl born in a place she didn't know and brought up by people she didn't know. Was she from the heat of the plains, from the waves in the seas, or from the highest mountains? No one knew, least of all her. But as she grew older, she belonged less and less in the world. The dancing lights of the Aurora was the only place she could be home.

'How she finds home, how she vanquishes the beasts she meets…that's what the book is about.'

'A fantasy for young adults?' I asked. I didn't know what he wrote. I'd assumed it was crime.

'Maybe… what do you think?'

He never answered directly, he always asked the same question back.

'If it's a fantasy, name her after me!'

'Maya! Why not?'

'Write about me,' I said imperiously.

'Always,' he kissed me.

∞

There were ways out. There were a dozen single men in my immediate postcode itself. I looked at my Tinder profile, tomorrow I would find someone else. I would forget Mark and move on. When he came begging me to have sex, I wouldn't.

Yet the next day, I was staring at the phone, waiting and waiting for his messages. I went out, met some friends, got stone drunk. Then I called him, once, twice, over and over again. The phone was on silent, later it was switched off. I left him messages. My eyes met a cute boy's in the crowd, greenish brown eyes, the way I liked them. I gestured and soon we were dancing. We went back to his, a few of us in a group. I sent Mark clips of the heavy breathing, orgasmic screams, made louder through editing. The boy was a student on holiday, he would leave in a few days, back to his native Greece. We promised to keep in touch. Perhaps we would. I liked him.

The next day, I followed Mark all the way from his home to the station. I did that for a few days but was careful not to be seen, even accidentally. After a few days of this I waited until the wife and children were on the school run and stood there, in full view, when he stepped out of the house.

He said he would file a restraining order. He explained the terms of a restraining order, and why I could qualify for one.

'But why do you think I'm stalking you?' I asked.

He didn't care, he said. He wanted me out of the way.

'I can expose you!' I shouted.

I could have, surely I should have torn apart that entire home with its pretty little porch, creamy beige blinds, the perfect shift dresses on his wife and the football kits on those boys. It was all in my hands to tear and ruin.

∞

Instead, I left. I came to Reykjavik. My first real home. My mother used to say, unrestrained nature had stitched itself onto me. When I was six, my parents moved to England but we still came back to Reykjavik every year for holidays. It'd become less and less frequent but the sting of the chill, the brutal fresh air had stayed with me. When London congested my very soul, this was the place I came back to. I liked being far away from everyone. Yet it wasn't easy being on my own. That's why I had gone back to the cutting, the criss-crossing, the delight of the blood falling in drops around me, on my feet at times. I said his name as I cut myself. Thin spidery ones, thicker solid ones. They healed but the steam room sometimes spilt them open.

I was supposed to have unbroken skin in this clean country with its steaming outdoor pools. I was supposed to heal in this city, with its surreal landscape. I was trying.

I wondered if Mark had healed.

∞

I had been quick in the darkness. I knew that he would come outside on a Thursday between nine and ten at night to put out the bins. Such a creature of habit, despite all his so-called creative impulses. I hid behind the English plane tree, branches expanding into the skies. When the side door opened, and he stepped out, I moved away to the back, then crossed the road. I approached silently, swiftly, then broke into a run. In my black hoodie I kept my head down. He looked up only when I was right there, a few yards away. Without staring into those eyes, I continued running and reached out just as I crossed him. The knife was sharp, I had focussed on how it would feel, how I would dig into his side, or maybe stomach, making sure it wasn't fatal but just a nice deep cut, enough to make him bleed. Just like the cuts across my arms and legs. I glanced only for a second to see the shock, the gasp which rose in his eyes, the terror which solidified in the whites. I assume he staggered and fell, perhaps he shouted my name, or screamed for help. I imagined the thickness of the blood, the redness on his legs, his clothes. Did he know it was my hand, did he suspect? I spent most of the night half expecting someone would come for me.

I left early for the airport early the next morning. Just like I had done in Rome. Only then, I had aimed a stone at Giovanni, and caught him on the head, as he walked back to his flat. In the darkness, he had never known.

∞

It's been a month here in Reykjavik and no one has come for me yet. Did he not suspect, or did he not tell?

I remember the time we had gone on holiday hoping to see the Northern lights. Every night, Dad would drive far out of the city. Every night, the clouds shrouded over.

I had arrived in their homes and hearts when I was four. I had been sent by the orphanage since they had arrangements with airlines to send children like me. My skin didn't seem Indian, they said. Where was I from, really? Maybe there was a Caucasian strain in me, given that I quickly felt at home, they said.

'You belong here with me,' Mark had said. I had never wanted to belong. The outside was where I was comfortable, where I could be as much or as less of myself. Where I stood and observed.

∞

Tonight, I would drive myself far away, along the snow-filled embankments, into the forests rife with frosted red berries, reindeer and wild bird songs. Once there, I would sit still and look up at the skies, waiting for the lights to break loose with abandon. I would bury myself in that chill and the freshness of those trees. I would stretch out on the bare earth, and push my body into it, the soil taking my shape. Above me I would see the Aurora flash, and there I would see home. No longer the other, no longer on the outside, I would be one.

That which is Unreal

All night the phone charges, and fills with messages, notifications, likes and pictures, so when Sandy wakes, there is plenty to browse. Duvet pulled up to her chin, she flicks icons and switches between WhatsApp, Instagram, Facebook, Messenger. Each of the apps bursting green and blue, read and unread messages, flitting on her phone like fireflies, glimmering bits of hope.

She scrolls down. Nothing still from Yusuf.

From R V:
Good Morning beautiful
        Morning
Miss you Sandy
        Nice
Can we video call?
        Not now. Will ping later

From S N:
Hi sexy Sandy!
        Hi
You are so gorgeous. Send me a picture
        Not now, am just waking up
Would like to see you in the raw. No filter
        ☺ Later!

Sandy gets out of the shower, steps into the outfit she laid out last night, and walks out, smoothie in hand. On the train, her fingers type slower, her messages more relaxed.

From Emily:
Hi babe

> Hey Emily! How are you? Been a while!

Am good babe. How are you?

> Haven't seen you for a long time on FB and no profile either?

Just had to be by myself. I dropped off FB. Now only on Messenger.

> All OK?

Ah yes. Therapeutic to be off. You tell me news? Any nice men?

> None, all virtual

What about that one? The man you think about. Nothing from him yet?

> You remember still? No…

Ah, no one and you so intense! You want them right there, isn't it?

> You know me so well, Emily! You should have been a man!

Yes, babe.

The train passes through Elmstead Woods, the bars vanish off the phone like always and the screen freezes. Sandy continues to look at Emily's profile picture. A fine boned wide-eyed pretty girl. Sexy.

Ever since Sandy's turned to canvas – she doesn't call herself an artist yet – she has this urge to reduce boundaries. To expand her very soul and connect with people, with the web of artists, poets, singers, musicians all over the world. That is why, some months ago, she modified the privacy preferences on her Facebook and has been accepting friend requests indiscriminately from strangers. She's opened an Instagram account and ticked it public. No limitations of knowing numbers or other details, anyone can get in touch with her. Many message her, more men than women, some real artists, some not, but all of them wanting to chat, telling her how beautiful she is. They are attracted by her profile picture they say, staring at the camera as if at a lover, her eyes wistful, her hair curly and shiny. And while waiting and watching her phone for that one message from Yusuf, Sandy finds there are so many others to interact with.

Emily is the mysterious one; her Facebook profile says: Lives in Paris, student at the Sorbonne, artist expression through watercolours.

But is any of that true? Once someone had contacted Sandy on Messenger:

Hello, how do you know Emily?

Just a contact. Why do you ask?

I want to warn you

About?

Emily. Don't think she is a woman. It's a man. Fake

profile. Tricking us girls.

> How do you know? Who *are* you?

Saw you are on her friends list. You from India right?

> Well many years before. I live in London

As another Indian I wanted to warn you

> I don't know her well. Like me she's an artist, sent me an invite

Be careful. She is a man. My friend and I have blocked her now

> OK thanks

Sandy had checked Emily's page carefully. Only two photos, very general posts. It could be a fake profile, and equally it could be genuine. She had contacted Emily immediately.

To Emily:

> Hi, someone contacted me to tell me you are a man. This is a fake profile

Isn't that funny babe? Why would I do that?

Emily hadn't seemed perturbed. She'd chatted instead about her boyfriend, passionate, intense, and how much she loved him, yet she didn't want to settle down. One man was no answer. Her questions, sometimes intimate, sometime searching. Sometimes a babe, you so special. Tell me, have you ever found a man who has been as special? Or: How long has it been since anyone has really held you the way you wanted it? Wouldn't you like to be dominated in bed? Many such messages over days and nights and with Emily's questions, as if a counsellor, as if an empathetic friend wanting to know her, Sandy had opened up, bit by bit, layers of onion. She had described Yusuf, the one under her skin, the one who doesn't answer anymore, the one whose messages she is waiting for. His voice, his touch, his body; what he gave and took. The memories as if stitched on, crocheted, knitted on her skin. Yusuf! The older boy who had helped her with her bag on the school bus the first day of fifth grade, when they'd moved from Delhi to Durban. The boy who was always at her side, from children to teenagers to adults, friend, lover, and now just an acquaintance like adults become after a certain age. The years past, and the memories that had grown in her, like ulcers and bumps.

∞

She hadn't told Emily how she now writes to Yusuf. Notes. Letters. In beautiful calligraphy, words in different colours. She likes to write on thick, handmade paper. She lets her fingers run over the unevenness of the cream surface. She writes on one side and on the other, she paints shapes, amorphous shapes she doesn't have any names for.

Yusuf, you see, it's all there inside me. I am sure you can feel it. Physically, like skin.

Look, I will try again. Scratch the surface, dig under the

skin, scoop out what you see inside. Don't you recognise it?

Look, just once. This mark here, can you feel it? It's not wild woman talk! This is from that day, fifteen years ago, when you had cupped a tear from my eye. You said cry as much as you wish, as hard as you need to, I am here. And I had, all night with the cicadas whirring and clicking, the jacarandas in bloom swishing in the breeze; my father, lying still lifeless in the living room. Everyone had wept all day and slept at night. Quiet and composed in the day, all night I howled drenching your sleeve; you didn't have a handkerchief and we didn't want to go inside to the kitchen to grab a serviette. All night I sobbed. All night you whispered to me, my tears seeping into you. That night, I knew Daddy had left forever.

Think of that other time, that pool party, wild like most of our parties were, that November evening in Cape Town? I was twenty-four, with happiness burning in my cells, the way it does when you think you have everything you possibly can. Roger had left my side, and when I walked into the garden, I saw him, in the corner of my eye, behind the house, and walking up to ask him if he wanted to join me in the pool, I realised he was not by himself, my boyfriend of four years was tongue locked with my best friend Evie. That look in their eyes, as if to say – you are so foolish, did you never guess?!

Love doesn't last forever, they said. Why did you think it would? This happens, live with it. And you seeing me, still like a statue in my white summer frock, came up to me, and said I had to ignore them. I was worth more. All night you let me cry, telling your wife you were caught up with work. Your wife, the one who owned you, a shadow so close to you, as if a part of you. I asked you if you needed to go back home. You said, I needed a home that night. I needed you more than your wife did. Those words are still stitched on me.

If you flip out all this skin, if you cut through the layers of adipose and muscle and bone, you will see it, won't you?

And that time, a year after, that afternoon, how did it come to be but lifting my top, you kissed my back. Those lips, the hint of a beard, soft stubble, rough nibbles; when the tongues lock, they needn't speak. We were in Kenya, on a safari, a group of friends together, wild outside. We had to tie ourselves to the bed, we had to be still so the other could ravage and explore, limbs and tongues. We had to manage animal-like, our human sensibilities, or was it our animal selves we had to lock away with human dignity? All evening and night we raged; poems and music were written, paintings were created while we lay spent, sweating, arms locked, lips locked, bodies locked.

You said, 'Jaan, it's not our time yet.'

In the morning, we saw the lions mate in broad daylight. Others took pictures, but we watched, imagine, I whispered to you, 'us.' That night we did it again, your tongue talking to me every way it could.

That night, those days, remain in me, dissolved in my blood, sometimes, rising up in small bubbles and forming blisters on my skin.

You can't not see all this. But still you remain silent. Over the years, I have known many men, been married once and broken up many times over. You have remained steadfast with your wife and family. Now, we are both free, and there's nothing else to disturb us, why are you silent? It is our time, if we want to be. Don't you see that, Yusuf?

∞

Her notes and letters pile up, a little stack next to her canvases, never sent.

Now they are both unattached. She is single. The wife has died leaving behind Yusuf and their child. Friends said her car skidded on the slope of the hilly path outside town and onto the path of a lorry. Sandy had messaged Yusuf when she heard. She wanted to go and meet him in Cape Town but he said he needed a break. Leaving the child with the grandparents, he was going to travel around the world and recuperate. England? No it wasn't in his itinerary. He wanted to be lost in the countries one got lost in: Bali, Vietnam, Cambodia.

Sandy still waits, in case he changes his plan to include England, the centre of the world, a quick visit? But nothing. Her WhatsApp messages to him remain double greyed for days, then turn blue, but there is no response. Even an innocuous hi remains unread for days. Sometimes a picture, sometimes a rare note to say, I am fine. In the hills today. Or an impassive how are you but nothing after that when she writes copious texts about how she is.

Instead, everyday a new man finds her. She reciprocates. Virtual love, fervent wishes to be lost in. When reality grows indefatigably like a maze of laurel, the virtual world with its half lights and quick promises soothes her.

From T.N:
Sandy, how old are you?
          Guess?
You are beautiful
          How old are you?
Twenty-five
          I am much older
You can't be more than thirty?

Thirty-four, she wants to say but doesn't. She chooses a different identity for these men who message her and want her. She becomes who she wants to at that moment. The words and pictures she sends are camouflaged, bits of a world with blue cell phone energy.

After work, in the evening, she goes for a run into the woods, her shoes pushing into the wet earth from the rain. Tropical signs from her childhood make their way here at times. The silence has been growing inside her, lush and verdant.

From C. K.
Can I call you? A video call. Please I want to see you.

Jaan. Sandy! Just once.

Jaan. The word is memory. Yusuf called her Jaan. He called a lot of people Jaan like people said darling or lovey in England. Jaan, life, my life. She is suddenly curious. She is at home; she can take a call.

C. K calls on Messenger.
A slight man sitting behind a large desk, a single plastic pen stand, some folders in front of him.

'You are at work?' she asks.

'Yes. And you responded, finally! I didn't think you would answer. Wait, let me go to the washroom. You mustn't speak. Ssshh.'

'What's up?' She notices his forehead is lined, as if he is having to think hard, do something very important.

'Jaan, please feed my hunger. Please release me. Open your blouse please.' He says this hand cupped on the mouthpiece.

'You are at work!' she laughs. 'You can't be serious.'

'I am serious. Please don't hang up. Will go to the washroom, don't say anything. Ssshh.'

She holds on, curious. He is walking down a dusty corridor, the phone bobs in his hands, and she watches the floor, untiled concrete. Then suddenly he is back in focus, gesturing silence, sash, Ssshh. The phone now hovering over his penis, pulled hastily out of his pants, his fingers on it, moving fast.

'Please, show me. Anything! Cleavage? Or show me your pussy. Please.' His eyes are desperate, waiting, as if he will see a miracle in front of him.

She obliges. 'Like this?' She lets the phone move over her. She slips her top down. She looks at him. He is smiling broadly, his eyes delighted now, saying Ssshh, grinning rakishly.

She hears it as well, a loud knock outside.

'Yes, yes coming,' he says. His fingers move faster. 'Please be quick. Show me more.'

She peels her jeans down. She is transfixed, amused, she is laughing. Ludicrous.

'Yes, yes,' he says and she watches him, as his fingers move. A yellow bucket stands at his feet, half-full. Buckets, so long since she has seen them, years ago as a girl in India. A mug on the side. Her own bathroom in England, such a contrast, beige-carpeted and clean. She thinks how in a few minutes he will pour the water over his flaccid penis and walk back to his desk as if nothing has happened.

Voices from outside again, 'Who is there? Come out!' Poor man, no peace in the bathroom, she thinks.

'Don't go, please,' he says. Wait, just a bit. Show me,' he is whispering, his fingers curled into a circle.

Then he hangs up.

At first, she laughs. She should be angry, affronted. How rude, how vulgar, how crass. She lies on the bed laughing, until she starts to retch and rushes into the bathroom. She throws up in the sink, a colourless dribble like the thin liquid spilling on his fingers.

Later she paints, loud vibrant colours on thick paper, and she writes.

Yusuf, Yusuf, you painted me once, in whorls, in swirls, numbing my boundaries and landscaping me. You watched me step out of my clothes, our fingers explored each other, our faces, our necks, our clavicles, one two three ten all along the spine, fingers resting at the base, especially that dip on your back. Do you remember?

Yusuf who doesn't respond and leaves her alone in this semi-lit world, leaves her alone searching, but who will she find in this un-reality? They seem to be free all day and night. Creatures hunting for women, from various places in different time zones, India, Egypt, Africa, Turkey, some older, some married, some single. What are they looking for? A free phone girl, titillate without payment; why didn't they watch porn instead of clumsy interactions on the phone?

C.K.'s desperate face remains in front of her eyes, a sad hunger lining the face. She checks and finds S.N. is online. She messages him.

S.N. is beautiful. Soulful eyes in a wide face, dusky skin, collarbones standing out stark, making her want to caress them. An odd desire to stroke his lips. S.N. is young, twelve years younger. He lives by himself in a 'one BHK' he says sadly, a one-bedroom flat in a small town in India. It's hot and his eyes burn every night. He wants to fuck someone, he says, but he craves soul and can't find anyone in the dust of his barren town, who connects with him like she does. Only she apparently can bring him the comfort he wants. His voice is familiar, it hides in her mind and she finds she can call on it when she wants to.

S.N. video-calls her. He plays on the guitar and sings, lilting Beatles songs. She could listen to him forever she tells him.

She goes for a drink after work the next day. They stand sipping glasses of wine on the riverside, poised perfectly, and watch the sun go down on the Thames, its waters gold and pink. The usual conversations, work, holidays, families and schools; the questions are the same, the answers as if pre-recorded. She isn't able to check her phone much since everyone is talking, really talking, face to face. They are nudging and joking with each other. The girl who sits three cubicles away from her is flirting with the boy who sits opposite her. After three reds, Sandy leaves, walks to her flat, and once inside, throws off her shoes, stands bare feet by the window, hands on her phone, her fingers moving fast on the keys, responding to all the messages. She looks up briefly between sending one message after the other.

A square canvas lies on the floor of her bedroom; she throws colours on it, thick red, and azure blue and then a grey and orange. She strips to a thin white slip, lies down and rolls herself in the liquid mix, skin and colour and paper meeting to form a shape she will later name and hang next to the other paintings on her wall. Coloured and with the paint dripping, she takes some pictures, to send later, maybe to S.N. C.K. is desperate for her pictures but she is avoiding him.

Every day, she thinks of Yusuf. The times they met, the times they hadn't. How he had such a traditional wedding, a nikah, followed every rulebook. She had been there with Will, her boyfriend at that time, had commented, 'Look at Yusuf! An arranged marriage, such a dutiful son. In this day and age! Spineless!'

In spite of the sarcasm, Will had asked, 'Did you fancy him?'

'Not at all. He was a just a good friend. You know, the ones who are sort of always there?'

She hadn't told Will how much she had liked it, when her fingers stroked Yusuf's arm, speckled with light golden hair, how she spooned him. She would never tell Will, she remembered every little detail of the five times Yusuf and she had made love, the clothes they wore, the way the rain drops had caught on the jacaranda outside the window.

S. N. hasn't been in touch for a few days. She has been checking his status and sees him online but there is nothing from him. She writes hello and he doesn't respond. The same person who called her so many times was he also ignoring her? She feels an anger rise, and writes.

To S.N.
Found someone else?

Not like that, Sandy!

Nothing after I sent that photo? Not good enough for you?

No, no, not like that at all

Then what is the problem

I am just feeling down

Why? What's up?

I wanted to ask you something…but

What's up?

Sorry but I thought you could help. Being in London. But I mustn't ask. I mustn't say it. Oh, I can't

What do you want?

Money. I want some money

What for?

I want to pay a broker to arrange a visa. I want to study in Australia. Anywhere abroad

Ah, right.

I am so selfish. I am sorry.

She's known S.N. for a month and half. She likes his voice. At times, commanding, at times, pleading. His eyes on hers, she wants to reach out and stroke his face. She has sent him poems, quotes, pictures. She wants to see him happy, and plans to buy gifts for his birthday. But money? She never expected the boy with the dreamy eyes would make such a request. She has some funds how easy would it be to transfer to him! But she knows she mustn't. She knows she should just delete him.

She has asked Yusuf again if she can come and meet him.
She misses him. A lot. Suddenly the phone glimmers.

From Yusuf:
Yes, but I am in Peru, too far for you.
> I can come there! Not far on a plane!
I will leave in a couple of days
> Where are you going next?
Brazil
> I can come there
Actually I change places every couple of days
> Well stay in one place a bit longer, and I can
> come. Wherever
OK, I will let you know
> When?
Soon
> Sure, that's great. I can take some days off
> not a problem at all. Just let me know

> When do you think you can let me know? A
> week?

> Shall I take some days off?

> Hi Yusuf, are you there? Let me know when
> I can come over

The messages stay double greyed. A day. Many days. A week. Many weeks. No response. She calls. No response. Sitting by the window, from where she can just see the top of the setting sun, giant yews blocking the rest, she thinks of how her fingers fit into the cleft on Yusuf's chin. How, when he smiles, it is as if he sees something right inside her, something he can't get enough of. Does he still miss a wife who doesn't exist anymore? Does he not want to see her, all of her? Does he not know how much she loves him, or doesn't he care? She waits, she thinks, she paints, she writes. She hopes. But nothing from him. He hasn't even read her messages. She knows he is there, she sees him online. She sends yet another hello. Then many more.

To Yusuf:

Are you alright?

I am worried now.

I miss you.

Don't you see? I really miss you.

Can I come to see you? I must see you.

One evening, a whole bottle of wine later, she calls. It rings but he declines the call. Tears running down her face she blocks him. He doesn't use Facebook much, but she unfriends him.

The next morning and the next and the next and so on, her phone wakes and everyone floats in as always, messages and lives together. C.K. begs forgiveness for his behaviour and sends her a poem but she ignores him. S.N. sings Coldplay's Para, Para, Paradise, we must find our paradise. She grows her list; P.M, P. L., A. G., even a W. U. More emerge from the half lights, initials she stores in her contacts. She messages Emily who assures her, you did right by blocking him, you enjoy babe. She has just gone through a break up and is looking for a new man.

Yusuf has been blocked for two whole days. Does he even know? Has he tried to message her? She knows she can unblock him any time. She heads to work phone in hand.

The Temple Cleaner

Shree Hingraj Mataji Mandir, Aden, Yemen

Nathu wakes at four a.m. every day. Outside he hears frogs croak, sometimes a faraway hoot of a night owl. He lies on his narrow cot for a few minutes, eyes open, staring at the ceiling. Spiders settle and weave their homes, and he lets the cobwebs form, dust clinging on the shiny threads. Until one day, he will pick up his long-handled broom and break their intricate homes, laughing to himself, watching the spiders carry themselves away on their long legs.

His room contains little else, the trunk, a durrie he has bought from the street market, an old chair with a threadbare velvet seat, his well-worn every-day slippers. The walls of the room are bare, shelf- less. The room itself, with a single window, is on the left of the narrow hallway. You climb thirty wide steps to reach the main doors of the temple, advance through the hallway, then step into the main courtyard, around which the shrines are clustered. Sometimes Nathu likes to sleep in the courtyard, in the open, under the stars. The bathroom is on the right of the hallway, and here Nathu washes himself, loud splashes, mug to bucket and bare body.

He's the temple cleaner, and for years his duties have been the same. Sweep, then mop the courtyard, the steps, all the way up to the inner sanctum of the goddess, the

84

Mataji. Then wipe the areas around the shrines of Shiva, Nandi, Ganesh, the gods themselves are lovingly washed once a month by Saravan, the priest, not by Nathu. Saravan is a Brahmin and Nathu is two levels below him, not an untouchable, but still not a Brahmin. It is Saravan who dresses the idols, patiently in their colourful fabric, yellow, red, orange, all bunched and tucked around their curves.

Today, before sweeping, he opens his trunk. He reaches into the folds of his only other kurta, light blue, and brings out his shaving mirror. He looks at himself, at the beard which covers most of his face. He curves his fingers on the shiny handle. He reads once more the letter from his son, then tears and crushes the paper into little balls. He lines them, unmoving ants, nowhere to go. Pushing the trunk back to its corner, he strokes the velvet on the chair. It is threadbare, but a small patch is still rich and soft like the sofas in his Dubai flat, years ago, that purple jacquard fabric. His mother had worried they were expensive. Indeed, it had consumed several months of his pay, but the look of opulence they brought to their flat! It had lighted his life.

'Live for the moment, enjoy and smile,' he used to advise his family. 'Kal kisne dekha?'

Who knows how many years have gone by? Six? Eight? Sometimes, when he goes to the Alsahareej, and looks into the water tanks, the face which stares back at him, from between the lotuses dotting the surface, seems unfamiliar. He often forgets he wears a brown temple cleaner uniform. Time, Samay, that elusive master – has stretched over his face, hollowed out his cheeks and scratched lines on his forehead.

The air of the Khusaf Valley is lighter than Dubai's. Even after all this time, he isn't fully used to it. Like every day, he begins sweeping from inside the temple, the dust fanning out in circles, then finally down the stairs, to the street. From dust to dust. He knows every tile of this courtyard. He knows the roughness of the edges, the bumps on the surface. The rhythmic swirl of the broom reminds him of the mornings in Dubai, in the flat, the girl sweeping under their feet as they ate breakfast at the table. The woman they had chosen for his wife, shy, dark-skinned, with large eyes and curly hair, married off with a little dowry. The match had been struck through some of their relatives in Mumbai.

His sister and mother decreed she couldn't enter the kitchen, being a mere bharwar, two levels below their own caste of thakarda. She could do chores like cleaning and washing but the kitchen would be out of bounds. Being in Dubai was a treat enough for her, his mother explained. The flat with its tiled floors and hot water. The gold she had been gifted. In Mumbai, what would her fate have been? She would have been married off to some slum dweller or walked the streets to provide for her family. His mother spoke sense, Nathu knew. But, sometimes, he felt sorry for the girl; when he saw her washing the toilets, when she dragged herself out of bed, after he had his way, or he flipped over her nightdress and she relented. She rarely spoke. They had two children, conceived right there on the bed, next to the room his mother and sister shared. He knew his voice carried over when he shouted, in spite of himself, in spite of the grimace on the girl's face.

The children grew up in the same room, sleeping between them on the double bed. After the children, she'd become even more inaccessible. She always had an excuse; an unwell child which needed nursing, a lightly sleeping child who might wake. He wonders now, had she cleverly planned to have the children, three years apart? Did she have her own agenda?

'Nathu, Nathu!' Saravan calls out, breaking his thoughts, 'You haven't started mopping yet?'

The sun has risen, and within an hour, grown hot on their heads. He knows he should have started the pocha. 'Am starting to,' he shouts back. Dip the cloth into a bucket of water, wring the excess water, wipe the floors with the wet rag. The temple's floors, made of white marble tiles as they are, prone to streaks of mud. Apprehensive about losing their footwear, people leave them in the car, walk barefooted in the sand, and sketch their footprints in the whiteness. He wishes they had a slipper-storage and feet-washing place like they do in Indian temples. He's heard of them. Erasing footprints in the dust is no easy task, he tells Saravan. In Dubai, he had a real job, unlike his brother-in-law, unlike anyone else in his family. He worked for a company repairing photocopiers in offices. When he mentioned this to Saravan, the retort was, 'Now you are just a temple cleaner. No more airs!'

But he remembers how rich he used to feel, when the money arrived every month in his bank account. Never mind that the money had gone before it came, in the pawns, the pledges, the loans. The purple sofa first, a pure wool carpet for the living room next. The girl reproached him sometimes, her eyes wide in worry, her mouth curved in anger. But he said it would be fine. There was always a way. The sister borrowed from him when she had her first child. Her husband decided to open an electronic repair shop claiming he knew everything about television sets and other appliances. But the shop had to be closed in a year, taking his money with it. He hadn't known housework in Dubai. With three women in the house, what was the need? The girl – he still thinks of her as a girl – his wife, did the menial jobs for years as commanded.

A Monday in 1967 they heard how those with British Protected Person status, or British Overseas Citizen status, could move to Britain. His sister and brother-in-law decided to leave, but he, Nathu, said he had moved country once – from Yemen to Dubai. Even though he lived in Dubai, he remained a Yemeni with a Yemen passport; when he retired, he would buy a flat and live in his own country forever. His sister protested, in England one could raise kids – well-fed, healthy, safe – then their protected status would be upgraded to British nationality one day. This was the opportunity one waited for, never to come again, they insisted.

He'd smiled, 'Kal kisne dekha?' I won't be a refugee in another country. I am wealthy, I will stay here. Apna khoon, my own blood living in my own home.'

His mother reminded him of the story of their family; how his father along with some of his friends, had voyaged from Mumbai to Aden on a ship. How they had carved a place for themselves and built their own community. Aden was ruled from Mumbai in those days, by the British. Indians often went to Aden, Indians often stayed back in Aden.

'We move, we leave to go where things are better,' his mother counselled. 'Your father came from India, he died in Aden. You, Nathu moved from Aden to Dubai. You brought me and your sister here. Now it is time to move from Dubai to England, and acquire a different passport, a renewed identity. We must leave.' He didn't agree. His mother went with the others, promising she would split her year in half, spend six months in England and six months in Dubai. She never returned. She died British, burnt in minutes in a retort, a nondescript cemetery in the north of England, ashes buried somewhere beneath the cold earth.

The girl eventually took her place in the kitchen and reclaimed her lost time by cooking vast amounts of everything; rotis, biryani, tandoori chicken, gajar halwa, anything the children asked for, anything she fancied. Around this time he had met the group of men from India.

They lived in a shared tenement and worked as labourers, builders, plumbers, electricians. They came to Dubai without families, without a society to embrace. With them, he saw a side of the city he hadn't known before, a Dubai he didn't know existed.

What had started as entertainment one evening continued over the weekend. The nautch girls were eager. Unlike the women he knew at home, their hair was oiled and fragranced; they sang ghazals, poetry of doomed, unrequited love, of Umrao Jaan. Noor, especially, his favourite. Jasmine flowers, smelling strong, circled their wrists. Bangles jangled. Pan laced their lips, and when Noor whispered to him, he waited for a faint spittle of red juice to slip out and land on his kurta. He shared his time and resources with all of them, they were his family.

As adults, his children were strangers to him. They'd both taken up small jobs, knowing they had to earn what they wanted to spend. The music which blared from their rooms was unfamiliar.

'This is English music. This is what the young listen to,' the son retorted.

The arrogance in the voice rankled. He'd strode into the room and switched off the CD. The son switched it on again. They went on this way, father and son looking into each other's eyes. His son towered over him. 'You are useless…,' and after a pause, added, 'Dad.'

Nathu had been left cowering.

The daughter took a man from outside. Not a Muslim,

not even an Asian, she selected a gora, an Englishman. Nathu had seen the man once, he was on the balcony, smoking, and the man had come to drop off the daughter. He saw his arms circle the daughter's waist, he saw him almost lift her up as they kissed, and he saw him set her down, gently. They didn't notice the glow of Nathu's cigarette as he stood there and smoked to the last puff. Later the wife said, 'Neena thinks Brian will ask her to marry him. He is from their England office.'

After two days she said, 'Do you know? Neena is now engaged. She says she will get married very soon.'

He knew he could say nothing. Like the son, the daughter would also defy him.

The gora expected nothing as dowry. It wasn't in their culture. The daughter decided to convert and become a Christian. She wore a white wedding dress which she bought with her own money. A small cross glistened on her throat as Nathu led her up the aisle in his old brown suit. He tripped just before the altar, and she hissed angrily, 'Can't you walk steadily? Just for today at least?'

It was a year or so after the daughter's wedding, that the manager called him in. He pointed out occasions when Nathu had been late for an appointment or hadn't been able to complete a repair satisfactorily. Nathu said nothing in defence, spent as he was from the night before, and dreaming of the hookah and jasmine on Noor's hair. He was fired, the next month's pay given as a favour. In Dubai, you never gained a right to stay, never acquired a citizenship.

You needed either a company or you someone in your family to sponsor your stay.

'I can manage only one of you,' the son said. 'Only mother.'

He still remembers the lurch he'd felt in his stomach, even though he knew the inevitability of those words. The wife, forced to be powerless all her life, remained so and said nothing. The daughter was settled and was about to have her first baby. Nothing could be expected from her. The brother-in-law in England, now with his corner shop, ignored his plea for help, almost as if he had never borrowed from Nathu. Almost as if he had paid back his debts. They all let him go. Just leave. Die. Anywhere. They didn't care.

He'd returned to Yemen, but with nothing. He stayed with a second cousin. Then a relative, an old uncle, informed him of this job as a temple cleaner. The food and accommodation were free. It was perfect for a homeless person like him. Sometimes, out of familial pity perhaps, the children sent him money. When the envelope arrived – *Nathu, Temple cleaner, Shree Hingraj Mataji Mandir, Aden* – an address simple in form, he tore it open in haste. A cheque in dirham from the son in Dubai or pounds from the daughter in England. He cashed it in the community bank. The pounds always more welcome, but rarer.

Two months ago, an envelope had arrived from the son. Instead of money, it contained a request. The son was getting married. To continue sponsoring his mother, he needed to be living in a two-bedroom flat and he could only afford a single bedroom place.

'Can you provide for mother in Yemen?' The letter asked.

So the son had done worse than the daughter, marrying someone with no money of her own. All his promises, all the bravado of looking after his mother had been nothing. Like flame in the wind, dazzling for a minute, but gone the next.

He looked around at his home, the temple. His black trunk with his possessions – two shirts, two pairs of loose khaki trousers – his uniform. Hidden in its depths, the little treasures which shone into his life. He didn't really have to think for very long.

'No, I cannot,' he wrote back. 'You children need to do this much for your mother. It's your responsibility. Try to get a new job with a better salary or ask your sister if she can take her.' The daughter, always the fiercer protector of the mother. He remembered how she had shouted at him once. 'You use the house as a hotel, mother as your servant.' How she had told her gora husband, 'We have nothing, since father did his kal kisne dekha and squandered his life away.' The husband had smiled at an embarrassed smile at Nathu. They knew of his escapades, his evenings with Noor. He imagined his daughter, curled up in a patchwork quilt, in her warm house in England, lights flashing in their glasses of wine, requesting the white husband, to obtain permission to look after her mother. But would he agree? And if neither the son nor daughter could look after her, what would become of her, the girl he'd married, with the wispy hair and buckteeth his mother used to mock?

It was more than a month since the letter, and he hadn't heard back from the son.

Today's cleaning has to be immaculate as it is Friday and the day of the monthly Ayyappa puja. Mr Rao, one of the main sponsors of the temple wanted it done, just like it was in his native South India.

'This is the only temple in Aden where we have a daily puja to the shrine. If we can offer a monthly Ayyappa puja as well, we will be doing so much for the community,' said Saravan. He had explained Ayyappa was so special, being the son of two gods, Lord Shiva and Lord Vishnu. When Shiva was in a rage, Vishnu had taken the form of Mohini, to calm and eventually seduce him. When Nathu grinned at the story, Saravan declared, 'As long as I am alive at least, this temple will live, we will always offer this place of worship for those who want it.'

The Ayyappa puja had become part of the temple tradition. Every Friday, the small Indian Hindu community in Aden arrived in the temple. Nathu recognised many of them; from the time he'd been a trailblazer and left for Dubai, for dreams and riches. They'd stayed behind; with the passing years they'd accumulated money, built themselves houses. They'd amassed, he'd dissipated. He avoided meeting their eyes.

Like always, he doesn't join the puja today. He sleeps in

his room, out of sight. It is only after everyone leaves that he will step outside and sweep the entire temple clean again.

It is still early on Saturday when he hears Saravan call out. It is meant to be a quiet day, Saturday. The temple opens only in the evening.

Then there is a knock on the door. 'Nathu, Nathu!' Saravan's voice is deafening.

'What is it now? I am coming, wait!'

Saravan continues knocking.

'I said I am coming,' Nathu arranges his lungi over his legs and opens the door. The sun is so bright; he has to keep his eyes shut. He wants to go back to sleep. Wasn't it Noor, lying on a white divan who he had been dreaming of? He is not able to remember or grasp shreds of the dream.

'Have you found it?'

'Found what?'

'Mrs Rao said she had come to the puja wearing her most expensive kundan earrings. She can't find one of the earrings, she must have dropped it in the temple! She asked if the cleaner has found it, have you?' Saravan speaks in a hurry, he is sweating.

'No, I haven't. There are so many people. Someone might have picked it up and taken it.'

'This temple is not that crowded!' Saravan said, pointing at the cave, the mountains surrounding them. 'Mrs. Rao is very unhappy. We can't displease her. We are the only one in Aden to have a working temple, we are lucky. Look again!

Sweep the temple, inch by inch.'

Nathu nods. He sweeps the courtyard again. He wipes the floors of the inner sanctum. He cleans the steps.

'Nothing here,' he says. 'She has lost it somewhere else.'

'She insists it's here. It is precious she said. Her wedding earrings, some family heirloom maybe. Have you looked properly?'

'Yes, I have, I already said that! But why does she worry? She can get another one made by the jeweller. The Raos are so wealthy. How does the loss of an earring matter?'

'What if Mr Rao withdraws his donations? What if she blames us? What should I do?' Saravan creases his forehead and worries.

'Kal kisne dekha?' Nathu gestures towards the skies, 'I leave things to the One who knows all.' He points at the shrine, 'You lie prostrate before her. She will speak to you and show you the way. I have told you before, haven't I?'

The goddess in the temple spoke to him, he often said; when it was night, when the moon shone on the mountains and the caves, on the outside of the temple.

'I am the one who does all her prayer rituals, why doesn't she doesn't speak to me?' Saravan retorts.

'You don't give yourself up. You have to forget yourself to find God.'

'You stop lecturing Nathu and look for this earring. Look all night and day if you must but find it! Mrs Rao is convinced she dropped it here, she thinks it was after the archana. I know, check in the heap of the anjali flowers!

Maybe it got caught in the shredded flowers as she offered to Mataji.'

'Impossible!' Nathu says. 'How can the earring slip off, stay hidden in the petals and get flung by her at the goddess?' He laughs to show how ridiculous this sounds.

'Enough! Look carefully! I will check in the shrine,' Saravan says, walking off, his crisp white dhoti sweeping over his legs.

The sun has already set, the lights illuminating the courtyard in a wide arc have come on. It is only after Saravan leaves, dejected and worried, that Nathu comes back to his room.

Under the yellow light of the bulb Nathu opens his trunk. The kundan earring sits in the centre, on his clothes, the stone catching the evening light. There are other things. A ring. Earrings, shining gold. A satin pink hanky. A child's bracelet. A flower brooch. A broken silver chain. He lets his fingers close on it, an elaborate earring. Red rubies and white pearls cluster on the dangling bell. In the centre, a diamond shines with a deep brilliance. Beautiful. Solid. He can take it to the jeweller and melt it into cash one day. He can keep it safe in his box with the other treasures. Shiny precious gold. Like the goddess's crown. Like the gold bracelet he had found once, a small ring, to fit a child's finger. Like this kundan, heavy gold. He had seen it glint between the bristles of his broom whilst sweeping near the central pillar in the courtyard after the puja. His fingers had closed on it.

'Why are people so careless?' he wonders aloud. When he sweeps, he keeps his eyes open for bits of treasure other people lose, bits of their life they let go. He stores them, it's his collection, gifts he has been given to shine in his life. He needs to keep something safe for himself. He closes the trunk and decides to go to bed. Kal kisne dekha?

Inside the City

Here in Vegas, I feel like myself, glittering, shiny, beautiful, the way I am meant to be.

Outside, the heat of the desert is all encompassing but as we enter the hotel, there's a sweet cool smell, as if the air is sprayed with Chanel. 'I am already in love with this city,' I say, and Karan smiles. Men feel fulfilled when their actions make women happy! I know how to delight them. I do it without having to think. I know he is proud to walk into the hotel lounge with me. I feel his hands on my bottom – nice skirt, he says. I am wearing my mid-thigh Prada white skirt and my strappy DKNY hot pink top. He says he can't wait to get to the room. And I can't either, though for a different reason. If the outside is this grand, then what are the suites like?

Karan stays in the most luxurious hotels, but here, in this land of opulence, it's all at a different level.

In the room, deep grey soft pile carpets, the walls as if spun gold. The bed is vast and even though trademark hotel white, the sheets have a soft sheen. Silk. I lie back on the pile of pillows and cushions, sink into the softness, sigh, and as he watches, I spread my legs. He immediately drops his iPhone, he had been on his emails, and jumps into bed. It is so easy, I think again, as he lies on top of me. It is easy, I think, to keep them wound round my fingers. Karan likes it when I keep my shoes on. I am wearing the red Jimmy

Choos, a gift from him. Again that's something they like.

Karan is one of my best customers, one of the steadiest. I have been his escort for a couple of years now. He hasn't used anyone else in a while

'Did you enjoy it?' he asks, twenty minutes later. He touches my face briefly.

'I did, you were amazing.'

That's my usual answer. Sometimes he spends time on me but I know when he wants to and when he doesn't. It is my job to give him pleasure.

We unpack, change and go downstairs. I wear an impossibly short gold strapless dress.

'So Vegas,' he says.

He drops the room key. I bend to pick it. I know he's done it on purpose.

'Nice,' he smiles.

Long slim legs, spray tanned to perfection. I look at myself in the panelled mirrors. He does as well.

There was that time, when I walked down Knightsbridge, past the Gucci, Chanel, Jimmy Choos, Prada, stand in the London rain and look inside. I wanted to step in, become part of that elegance, have a handsome attendant wait on me, flash my card without a worry. As an au pair in Knightsbridge, my monthly salary wasn't enough to even buy a belt in one of those shops. Then I saw an advertisement by chance, an impulsive application to Carmen's Escorts and in a few hours, a request from them to send in photos or come in for a photo shoot. Though expensive, I wanted to have the photos done professionally. I put together my own outfits however, instead of taking up their makeup and accessories package. A diaphanous sarong worn like a dress, bunched at the waist with a bold belt, red and beige stilettoes I borrowed from my employer. She wouldn't miss it, considering she had an entire closet of shoes, and these were the ones she never used. We had a choice over exposure – face or not, full frontal or clothed, topless, a side back, full back and so on. I went for the complete sans the face. I sat coyly on a chair, legs crossed, wearing shoes. Only. In another, I wore my scarf dress, and they had a fan blowing from the front, my curves showed through the falling away fabric. I did a mini striptease with my bikini from New Look. With the heels, a large vintage necklace hanging on my chest, nobody would guess the bikini cost only a tenner. They put me on the medium range, two weeks trial, they said. If I didn't hook, I would be put on the lowest band of five hundred pounds for an hour. But Karan called up almost within an hour of my photo going live.

Later, he told me why. The hair and the almost-crazy dress sense intrigued him, he was sure the face behind the veil was beautiful, and he was impatient to see it. I hadn't agreed to my face being photographed, since I worried my employer or one of their friends might use Carmen's.

After a few months of being a high-class escort, I left my au pair position. The jobs demanded similar talents: to pacify. The hours were more demanding of course, but I could earn sky-high money. I could shop on Knightsbridge and build up a collection of clothes faster than my employer.

Karan orders some Cristal.

'May I?' he pours some into the crystal cut glass.

Of course. I never say no to champagne and certainly, I never say no to anything he asks. He had sensed that from my poses. A strategically shown backside, enrolled in the duo section, I had given out messages that I was out there, ready to put out, in, out, anywhere.

Initially he sent me out with his customers. When he wanted to close a deal, there I was, trussed in low necklines, a single ruby or diamond nestling on my chest, my skirt or dress so short that I couldn't sit down without showing my jewelled knickers. From dinner dates to theatres to night sex. The old Indian man who awarded Karan the multi-million deal, and made me stand in various poses, in my shoes and jewellery. As a thank you, Karan had taken me shopping. Later, I said I'd felt nauseous just watching that man drool over me, and still later that night, he said he wouldn't send me out anymore. I was his. But he forgot the promise. I was out with a Japanese man, who expected geisha behaviour. I was demure, coquettish, fully dressed, but with no underclothes. Fetishes, desires, lust. I went with it.

'Would you come with me to India?' Karan asked once.

'Why not?'

I had travelled with him all over Europe and sometimes

102

to the US, like now. Sometimes he used Daisy, who was from Czech. But I feel his background, his past from India, would always remind him that beauty was about being dark skinned, dark haired. His fascination with blondes would always be momentary. We Hispanics are warm and passionate. I told this to my clients if I ever felt I was losing out with my looks and curves.

'In Indian clothes… indeed, you could even look Indian. Like a mixed Indian. I could introduce you as the British Indian friend. Yes, why not?' he said.

∞

Dinner over, we walk back to the Venetian. We watch the fountains flash and dance in Bellagio, then we hear strains of music from The Mirage.

'A.R. Rehman,' he says with a look of absolute delight. I know that composer. I have studied all aspects of popular Indian and British culture to keep up with Karan's dual identities. We move on, cut through crowds waiting for the pirate show, children on their fathers' shoulders. It is strange to see so many families in Vegas. We sleep early, still a bit jet lagged. From tomorrow onwards, my days will be about the gym, the spa, shopping, and entertaining all evening at Karan's high-powered dinners.

In London, in the roof gardens, which we visited often, he had told me about the girl from India. A faint fragrance of roses and lilies merged with the grilled sea bream I was eating. The girl was from one of the premier business families. Marrying her meant a further increase in his dominion with offices in Singapore, China even. He could grow his business without acquisition or organic growth.

'You don't have to justify your decision, least of all, to me,' I said. Even I could hear the agitation in my own voice.

'Are you upset?' he asked, calm as always. He meditated every morning to control his mind. The Indian wisdom layered with the English sangfroid. It was a winning combination. No one could faze him. And at that time, I had wanted just for once to see his power drop, just for a minute the beautiful expression he wore to change.

'Not at all!'

'You sound it.'

'Why would I? I am a professional – just like you.'

'Bella, Bella, Bella,' he said theatrically.

'Can I get some more of the Chardonnay?' I wasn't worried about losing his business. There were others. I was popular. Besides business improved at times after they got married. Bored with the wife at home, they went out on longer trips, hosted more events.

When we returned to his Porsche, he held my hand. 'Really, are you not upset that I may get married? The proposal has come to my parents. It is tempting... all those companies.'

I caught a whiff of the garlic in his breath. He often smelt of it.

'No, not at all,' l laughed.

He looked puzzled, then suddenly he said, 'Marry me.'

'The Indian girl?'

'No, you. I am asking you.'

How could he propose, without a ring, without being on one knee? I had dreamt several times of my first proposal but it couldn't be this. Racing though the drizzling, hazy streets of London, the thought of another girl in his mind, garlic in his breath. Was he pulling my leg?

'Is that your proposal?' Perhaps my voice sounded more sarcastic than I intended. The moment changed in a second. Like a glass shattering. Like seeing a rainbow one minute and then nothing. He turned to look at me.

'No, of course. You would want it all, the trappings, the diamond… of course.'

Katy Perry sang Roar. I preferred it to the classical music he liked.

That night we hardly spoke, but I know it was one of the best he had. He had been rough, raw, and I responded in fervour. Was he angry? But if he was serious about me, surely he should have planned it, not blurted marry me whilst driving, expecting me to take it seriously?

I didn't meet him for a week after that. Carmen's sent me out with someone who paid double, some Arab businessmen who were visiting London from Dubai. They chose a few of us in a group. They enjoyed seeing us dance together, our hips twining and coiling into each other. We had to take the initiative with them. Initially reticent but after a while, very lecherous.

Then Karan called me about Vegas. Nothing to refuse.

Except that when he kept making those calls to India, to that girl, I found myself getting annoyed. Once I answered his mobile and heard her voice.

'Jaanu,' she said.

'Hello?'

'Who's speaking? Can I speak to Karan?'

It's me, the girl he's with. The girl who's been at his side all year. I handed the phone to Karan without saying anything.

I spend the morning in the shops. I choose a $600 Vera Wang, dark purple dress, cut to my navel. The woman comes back all flustered saying there is a limit on the card. It's the add-on card Karan had gifted me.

'There never was before,' I snarl at her.

'I am sorry, there is now,' her smile is frozen. She is used to this, perhaps.

I understand. I am not stupid. Karan is reducing my expenses. Maybe he wants to buy something like this for the girl from India. The thought of that girl squeezing herself into a dress like this is ludicrous. I had seen her photos. Her chest was large. She would spill out of this low-cut dress.

'Never mind,' I say and swing out of the shop. I am angry. The half-meant proposal I had ignored. The girl who keeps messaging and calling him. A slow panic rises in my throat. Without Karan, I will have to go back to ad-hoc jobs. It will take years to find someone like him. This girl who hardly knows him will get it all.

∞

I don't bring up the incident at dinner. Delicate scallops as starters, duck comfit, a Shiraz. My dessert is orange cream in dark chocolate.

We walk back in the heaving night. The sprayers are still on, even at midnight the heat emanates from the desert air. The lights shine pink, blue, orange. Colours. Smells. Sights. I love this city, I tell him.

'We can come here again,' he smiles holding my hand.

I want to ask how. When he is married, will he still meet me?

'Maybe for New Year's Eve?' I ask.

He doesn't take the bait.

'If you like it so much, why not?'

His phone rings. It is her. She calls him so often.

I walk ahead, lose myself in the crowd, the fountains are dancing in Bellagio.

It is only when the show ends that I start looking for him. Where is he? Has he gone back to the hotel without me? What if he doesn't let me back in tonight? Tells me to leave?

I start running through the crowds, pushing a few people, looking at every face. Where is he?

I hear his whisper, 'Bella...'

And there he is, standing against the wall, looking at me all the while. I smooth my hair, regain my composure. We hold hands and walk back.

The slot machines are alive, shining, in the lounge. He pulls me into one.

'Let's gamble.'

He wins. Every time. He gives me the money to buy something from the shop in the Venetian. I choose a faux diamond-jade ring. Will this be his last gift to me?

In the lift, I stand close to him and say, 'I will miss you.'

'Are you leaving me now?' he sounds like he is mocking me

'I mean, when you do. I will never leave you. It's not like me.'

'Would you not?' he laughs.

That night we make love. I want to feel him, taste him and know him. I am not thinking like an escort anymore, not holding back. Is it too late for me?

I whisper 'If only I could bring that moment back.'

'Which one?' he asks between shudders.

'You know… that night, in the car, after dinner in the Roof Gardens. When you asked me?'

He looks surprised. As if he can't remember.

'On an impulse. I didn't know then,' he says, after he finishes.

'What didn't you know?'

'This isn't real. You aren't real.'

He falls asleep in a minute. I sit on the gold sofas and look out of the windows. The fake city shines in the desert. They make cities like this, they make people like me. Perfect on the outside but only because they have been constructed, brick by brick, cell by cell, hair by hair, not evolved, not experienced.

I see his phone flash, on the bedside table. A WhatsApp message. I type in his passcode. She's sent him a picture. A red halter dress – Jaanu, how do I look? Thinking of you, miss you. Kissing emojis. Her face! Garish red lipstick not applied properly. Her bust line doesn't work in the halter. Wobbly things. She needs to tone down, severely tone down.

Karan is asleep on his side, his face away from me. I type – Red doesn't seem your colour. I have seen better. Also try some workouts, babe!

Even as I am thinking I shouldn't, I press send. I wait, a breath caught in my throat, in case she calls. Nothing. Silence. Karan's steady breathing. I wait, then click on both messages, and delete for me. I get into bed, close to him, put my arm around him, and sleep.

In the morning, our cab arrives. The driver is from Ethiopia. People often ask Karan where is he from. They feel a kinship perhaps. Within minutes, we know the driver's life story. How the US government requests for workforce from other countries, how they processed his papers, how he bought his cab and how his children are being educated so that they will never starve ever like he had. How he is eternally grateful to Vegas.

Karan is fiddling with his phone and frowning. He calls repeatedly, but the person on the other end keeps hanging up.

'Never mind... women,' he mutters and looks out at the still sleeping city.

'Problem?' I ask.

'Nothing which can't be sorted out, am sure,' he says in his usual calm voice.

The driver continues. Vegas is his lifeblood. People come here for amusement but not him.

'Even Vegas has a heart, eh?' Karan laughs. He looks into his wallet and pulls out a wad of notes, signalling me to give it to the cab driver.

'He expects a tip,' he mouths. 'Will help him a bit.'

Five hundred dollars. Four times the fare. Even Karan has a heart. He will find out. He will know it was me. Will he then want to know the real me, the real reason I sent that message?

Our cab speeds on. Here in Vegas, I am a different person. Here in this shining city I see myself, shivering, lonely but true. I sense our hearts. I sidle closer to Karan and hold his hand.

The Golems of Prague

Today

Ivana dresses with care; she rolls her hair and spritzes it. She has worn her black skirt, fitted tight on the waist, frilled taupe top tucked in. Her nails shine a bold coral pink. A part of her protests: the golems won't know whether you are dressed to the hilt or not. But she feels safer behind this immaculate appearance. Such an important day after all. Finally, the golems, the robots, are here. Months of designing solutions, project plans and contract discussions have climaxed into this chilly autumn morning. Audra has run out of the front door minutes ago, her long legs taking her swiftly to the school bus. Now that Audra is fifteen, cocooned in an attitude of independence and indifference, Ivana has extra time on her hands.

The day hangs tent-like, the sun half appearing within the clouds. She steps out of her front door, digs her forefinger into the pot of red geranium to check – nicely damp, doesn't need a drink – then walks five minutes to the bus stop. A two-minute wait, and in the bus, from her usual seat, outlined through the window, she watches the tourists on Charles Bridge. Selfie sticks rise in the air like small birds, photographs clicked every minute. She watches the statues on the north side of the bridge come into view, one by one. There is Vitus, face downwards, standing on the rocks, lions at his feet, and for an instant, she can almost see Hans – stop, look at her, tip her face, kiss her. Then it feels distant; the solidity of his touch, a memory questioned.

Some months ago: She and Hans, walking arm in arm; two lovers stopping at every sculpture, admiring, taking pictures; him of her, him of them, him of the city spread-out accepting, waiting to be explored just like her. He stopped by the Vitus to kiss her.

'Why here?'

'Why not?' She has one picture, the sun, a deep orange ball, sinking into the waters, their silhouettes, lips meshed, tongues entwined, smiles frozen. She stares at it on lonely evenings. She has lost count of the number of times he has flown between New York and Prague, the number of days they have spent together.

It was on Hans's visit last December that they first heard about automation and artificial intelligence. Hans was a senior manager from the American head office, visiting other office locations across the world, and educating them about the benefits of using automation at work. Prague was his first stop. He talked about software robots, how they could be rolled out in the organisation to do jobs in departments such as finance and accounting. How the robots were clever enough to read handwriting, how they could self-learn from the past month's work, and apply it to the next month. Clever, like humans.

She'd invited him to the Christmas dinner party, not sure if he would accept. But he agreed readily, and they walked to the restaurant together. It was dressed up like most of the city, a festive wreath hung over the entrance, a tree glimmered in the corner, a multi-coloured mix of stars, bells and drops. She ordered Svarak for the table, and warming her hands on the glass, listened to Hans, seated next to her, their legs almost touching. By the time the starters were served, he had moved from the topic of work to playing truth or dare. Drunk and happy, they laughed all evening, and catching his eye when they did yet another bottoms up, Ivana suddenly felt special. That night was the first time she had allowed herself to follow a man she didn't know well enough, to his hotel room, but Audra was at a friend's and she told herself it was a festive time after all.

Later, he said there was no way he could have refused an invite from the elegant, sexy lady dressed in red. He said the lights had shone on her, her skin golden.

The morning after they had breakfast together in the café near work. They sat at the farthest table, at the corner of the bar, tucked away from the other guests, and Walter, one of the waiters she knew well, gave her a little wink of approval. The latticed window looked out on the winding cobbled street. Hans ordered an egg and avocado sandwich, and she a buttery croissant. Over two cups of coffee each, they exchanged as many life anecdotes they could, to know more about each other, than their bodies already had.

After a couple of months, others joined Hans. A team arrived from an Indian consulting company to analyse and decide what processes could be handed from the humans to the robots. Meera and Hitesh, a business expert and a technical expert, two peas in a pod, a splash of black hair and brown limbs in their white and blonde office.

'The robots will do everything faster, much more efficiently,' Meera said.

'But what exactly is this robot?' Ivana had a vision of a little R2D2 walking next to her helping with the daily accounts.

'It's just software we develop. Initially we used to install our software, 'robots' on laptops and desktops, a single robot could do the tasks of five humans or more. But they could only do very simple tasks, which involved no thought. Now, we have made them cleverer, we have allowed for the robots to machine learn...' Hitesh said, his glasses glinting. Hitesh added a layer of technical detail to whatever Meera said.

'Robotic Process Automation and Artificial Intelligence' Hans cut in, sounding nothing like the man who had learnt and then whispered in Czech to Ivana. The man with a voice of silk who had whispered yesterday evening – 'chybíš mi, chci tě misto.' I miss you, I want you good.

'Ivana! I had explained everything to you all, hadn't I?' he continued, 'We can build this intelligence so they can do your work more efficiently.'

'Since robots don't ask for holidays and work 24/7,'

Meera added with a smile. Titters in the room. Ivana's own laugh was loud but forced.

'They need a laptop but no seat,' Hitesh smiled.

Later at lunch, as she sliced her avocado half into quarters, she thought of the legend of the Golem, the bedtime story her grandfather used to tell her. Long time ago, the Rabbi of Prague, Judah Loew ben Bezalel, also known as the Maharal, summoned the four elements to make a magical creature. The Golem was formed to protect the Jews. At first wordless and subservient, he helped the Rabbi with household tasks, gradually he grew stronger and cleverer, until one day he couldn't be controlled anymore. One day, he overpowered his own creator. Her grandfather's voice would fall silent, and then rise louder, as his hands waved to show the destruction the Golem did. He bought her a clay Golem. She kept it in her large yellow box with her wooden puppets.

As Hans, Meera and Hitesh discussed the robots, forks clanging on the white plates, hands gesticulating, Ivana's worry took the form of the Golem. It screamed to her: if the robots needed laptops and no seats to work at, it meant the ones who needed the seats wouldn't be needed anymore, they would lose their jobs.

She asked, 'What happens to my team if these robots take over our work?'

'Oh, free your staff to do more creative things. Take the robot and routine out of a resource,' Meera said, eyes almost misting away in earnestness. Dark-haired Meera with kohl-lined eyes, plum lipstick accentuating a perfect mouth. So exotic, thought Ivana, the word sitting on her tongue like a sharp taste of mango chutney she'd had in an Indian restaurant. Meera, Hitesh, Hans, heads together, earnest, as if discussing world peace. The chandelier with its spidery arms covered their table in a soft glow.

Outside, the winter sun was beginning to set, it would be dark by the time they went back to the office after this long lunch. This café was her spot, where she came to have a coffee and spend a half hour, lost in the sounds of the beans frothing in the machine, or brought the team to celebrate and infuse their ordinary days with something special. It wasn't meant to be the kind of place you added to your routine like Meera and Hitesh had done, with Hitesh claiming this was the only place in the vicinity of the office he could find something to eat – I am vegetarian you see – and Meera claiming she liked the variety. He always ordered the wild mushroom risotto while Meera flitted over the menu like a butterfly, choosing differently each time.

She didn't mention any of her thoughts to Hans that evening. They never discussed work. Hans careful perhaps of the seniority. She, not wanting him to think she needed any favours from him. So, she suppressed her golem worries. The moments with him had to remain perfect, unclouded.

They had a ritual. They spent evenings together; a concert, a restaurant, a walk along the Vltava, and sometimes in his room when he had to attend to work calls.

Brown hair licking over his forehead, face intense as he spoke to clients, she felt somewhat maternal towards this man, ten years younger. All new American blended with old German heritage, and modern global in his habits.

'Do you have a woman in every port?' she teased.

'Only you,' he answered, call over, his fingers trailing her bare back. He was always so hungry. Through the large window, curtains drawn back, she watched sunset colours change the skies, as he held her, stayed inside her like no one had for years.

In August, Hans said he didn't need to come back the next month. Other countries and offices were on his list, Russia, Philippines, Brazil.

She wondered if she should give him a goodbye present.

'I love Prague. I will come back on a holiday, just to see you.'

'Once more at the café?' she messaged him on the last day. She had wanted a coffee, a drink, dinner, the bed back in his hotel. A see-you-soon whispered between the sheets.

'Of course,' he responded but invited Meera and Hitesh as well, who asked others.

'Not the same café,' Hitesh said. 'Let's go somewhere else today.'

'Sasazu? Retro? Lucerna?' The names fell off Meera's tongue as if she was the one who had grown up in Prague, strolled her streets as a lover, as a mother, as if she was the one who belonged here.

'All three!' laughed Hans bundling them all into taxis.

In Lucerna, Meera drank red wine, glass after glass filled by willing hands, Hitesh sampled beers. Ivana sipped her vodka and watched the group dance, refusing to join them saying she was tired. All of them happy, hand in hand, shoulder to shoulder, gyrating, bodies touching. Ivana shut her eyes and let the music drum in her mind. After some time, when she said she wanted to leave, Meera rose unsteadily, 'Enough of dancing, I must head back.' But Hitesh wanted more. 'The night is mine,' he laughed, heading back into the dance area with one of the other girls.

Hans ordered taxis for both and offered to drop Meera back in her hotel.

'Safety first. Meera's in no state to go on her own,' he whispered to Ivana. She nodded and got into her taxi, there was nothing else to say. She slid down the window and reached out to touch his hand. As the cab drove off, she pushed her fingers on her lips, as if to hold on to a sense of him but felt nothing. She realised she hadn't asked when she would see him again.

After all, nothing had been promised.

Things got busier after that. Ivana found herself on calls with teams in India who were building the software, sometimes very early in the morning due to the time difference. She had to explain all the processes, all the errors which may occur so that the intelligence would be built into the robots and they could work like Ivana and her team did. She made excuses to avoid the calls.

'I need to meet a friend in hospital.'

'Audra has something at school today.'

'Don't you get it, Ivana? If we don't help, we will be out.' Igor sighed, 'You have to co-operate with Hitesh and Meera.' He was the head of the unit.

'Do you understand what's happening? They are here to get rid of us!'

'You are only giving them information of the processes Ivana, nothing more.'

'I am telling them what I do, so that they can do it. They will automate the process and get a golem to sit here doing our work. Ten golems sitting neat in a row, chugging away all day. And night. Since robots don't need holidays.' She said that in an exaggerated Indian accent.

'Golems in a row? Ivana! What are you going on about? Listen, these robots, I mean all this software may not even prove as efficient as they think. As of now, just focus on the project and give the Indian team whatever information they need.'

The golems would be under observation for a month, not the usual three-month probation period new employees had to go through. Just a month of no-error comparisons and validations, and the golems would get to stay for life.

Hans hadn't written or called since he left. Ivana emailed him once: Meera has asked for details of my team members, the first five to lose their job, do you remember them Hans? Do you? There was no response for two days and then finally an email to say – Hi Ivana, glad the initiative is going well. As you know the organisation is embarking on a process of transformation and embracing artificial intelligence to work along with human creativity, Best, Hans. It was a well-crafted response from a corporate executive, not that charming man who had held and shuddered into her, so many times, in that quiet light-soaked room in the stately Hotel Wandl. She wanted to scream, to reply, write normally, call me! She stared at his photos on her phone, she wanted to call him.

For generations Ivana's family had woven cloth; strong squares of linen, delicate laces. Then the machines arrived. As the looms took over, churning yards of fabric, quicker than human fingers could, the family had to give up weaving and seek other jobs. Her grandfather had told her, 'They could take away our cloth since our hands can't match a machine's speed, but our minds! No machine can overcome the brain. If you live in the world of letters, no one can displace you. You must be educated, Ivana, and have a job, a real job.'

So Ivana worked hard, rows of numbers queuing in her tidy brain. Her desk orderly, papers stacked over each other, pens and pencils arranged in a partitioned box. She graduated as an accountant. Now, a senior manager dreaming of bigger global teams to manage. All that was to come to nought since Golem-like, these software robots would soon take over, and Ivana and others like her, would lose their carefully built up lives, their present turning into bleak futures. Everything was to come to nought thanks to people like Meera and Hitesh. And Hans.

Today

On this chilly autumn day, Ivana walks fifty steps from the bus stop to the office, pausing for a moment to buy a few bags of trdelnik, just a little something for the team in the morning meeting. She will place the paper bags in the middle of the table in the conference room, next to the phone; they will tuck into the soft dough, the fine white sugar catching their lips, a fine dust settling over on the polished table, the smell of the spice like panacea. They will then wait for the green signal that the robots were working. Within four weeks, if all goes well, Ivana will need to make five of her team members redundant. The numbers will increase over the next few months. Every month, she will have to fire some more, and then finally Igor will fire her. She is sure of this.

At ten a.m. the program is switched on. The robots are here.

Meera sends her an email – lunch, same place?

Ivana agrees. By the time she arrives, Hitesh and Meera are already at the café, sitting near the entrance. The bar isn't busy. Walter waves at her as she sits down.

'Red or white? It's celebration time!' Hitesh says.

She notices they already have a bottle between them, so she politely says, 'Red.'

'Our robots have been busy, Ivana,' Meera says. 'About five hundred records have already been processed. Your guys can relax now.'

'How exciting,' she says. Relax. Yes, with the jobs gone, they can relax.

'You will earn a big commission this quarter, won't you Meera? This deal was a sexy one,' Hitesh says. 'Party when we get back?'

'Any time.'

'Dinner in the Shard then, when we are in London. It's on you! Hans will be there as well, isn't it?'

Meera makes a mock angry face then says, 'Yes, Hans is in London this week, so let him pick the tab! He said he owed me one.'

'Hans is in Europe?' Ivana's voice is faint even to herself.

'Think so, that man is always travelling! Wonder how he does it…'

'But, hey we should party here isn't it, go out with Ivana,' Hitesh goes on.

'Yes, good idea, why not tonight? We will do another one in London with Hans.'

Ivana doesn't smile back at them.

'I am busy tonight, maybe tomorrow,' she says, except that she isn't. All she will do is go home, sip her Becherovka and pore over the bit of lace she has been working on. Audra is away at a friend's. Hans is in London, a two-hour flight away and he hasn't even told her.

'Nah, we are leaving tomorrow,' Hitesh nudges Meera. 'Tonight has to be the night.'

'Next time then, Ivana,' Meera smiles that consoling smile of hers.

'If there is one,' Ivana blurts.

'Of course, there will be. We won't forget you, Ivana! I will come back and see you.'

'Why? To take away the rest of the team? Take my job as well? Haven't you done enough?'

For a moment there is silence, broken by a loud gulp as Hitesh drinks his wine.

'It's not like that all …people can be redeployed you know,' Meera says. Ivana wants to laugh – a bit of camembert is stuck between Meera's pearly teeth. 'But you know what? I will miss Prague; I will miss this strange little cafe. It just feels so… you know… comfortable? Like home! Isn't it just amazing, to come to another part of the world, and feel at home? You know?' Meera looks at Hitesh first, and then Ivana, waiting for them to agree.

'Where will my team be redeployed? Where exactly?' Ivana's voice is high.

'Oh, they will find other jobs, better jobs. Artificial intelligence works alongside human creativity.' Meera has learnt her sales pitch well. Meera with the camembert stuck in her teeth, Meera with the shiny shoulders and brown legs casually placed so close to Hitesh's.

'Do you know robots make the best surgeons, even customer care assistants? Soon, they are going to be used to deliver food in London. Everything can be automated. It's the future,' Hitesh chimes in. 'It's cast in stone.'

'Aut-oma-tion., Auto-ma- tion is here to stay, the robots are here to stay, auto-mate every day!' he suddenly sings.

'What about trying to automate your own jobs? Make yourselves redundant?' Ivana asks.

'Ours? Why not! Ha Ha!' Meera laughs as if it is very funny.

'Yes, it can be done but not our kind of solution selling. And, anyway who can automate Meera?!!' Hitesh says. 'I mean, someone like her! Look at her!'

Meera turns towards Hitesh, places a finger on his arm – a slender finger with a flower-cluster ring – and laughs loudly. Ivana wonders if they have known each other's bodies before. Has Hitesh's flabbiness lain on Meera? Have they been spending evenings together as well? And what about Hans? She pictures Hans's trim golden body on Meera's. Drop her back in the hotel in a cab, walk her upstairs, unbutton her out of her polka-dotted blouse. Hans, head of artificial intelligence, congratulating Meera, this newfound automation queen. Congratulating and going down, on her. Once and then again, meeting in London, meeting in India...

It is easy enough. Without planning the trajectory of actions, without a thought, Ivana tugs at one edge of the tablecloth. It shifts, the bottle of wine rolls, the Beaujolais drips on Meera's cream dress or maybe it is beige, no doubt from an exclusive shop in Paris or London. The spicy red notes of berries quickly stain Meera's legs – so the smoothness isn't her own her skin, it's only some expensive tights! Meera says 'Oh my God' and stands up. Hitesh's mouth falls open, and for a moment he really looks like that orange fish in her parents' aquarium, the one glued to the glass, staring out, its mouth opening and shutting in large circles. It makes Ivana laugh. It is hard to stop.

Then Meera asks, 'Ivana, are you all right?' her large eyes contorting in worry, as if she really cares. As if she cares.

No, she isn't all right, and she doesn't need to be.

'You are no Maharal! None of you fucking lot are!' she shouts. She jerks the red and white checked fabric, thinking how similar it is to the disposable one in her own flat, on which Hans once doodled hearts. Their pasta bowls crash to the floor. A few clams nestle in Meera's spaghetti, Hitesh's mushroom risotto is an untouched heap. The chilli-flavoured olive oil bottle shatters into a thousand slivers. Ivana steps over the chillies, steps over the perfect white circles of mozzarellas from her own salad and walks straight to the wooden doors. She feels the waitress's eyes on her back, sees Walter rushing to the door, and imagines Meera wide-eyed, deep-kohl-line eyed staring in shock, Hitesh's hands on hers, stroking her, consoling her.

Ivana caresses the gargoyle locker, for luck they say.

Later, they will say she has lost it. Later, these robots will not work perhaps, disintegrating into meaningless code, like the fine grains of earth her clay Golem had turned to. Later, there will be an email from Hans explaining artificial intelligence is only there to help human creativity. She knows none of it is true. She is sure the Golem will do what it does, it will stop them all, destroy them, even Hans.

She doesn't look back. She walks fast, her heels strike the

cobbled streets like drums, like music. A gentle rain falls around her, on her hair, on her shoulders, like woven lace.

Fitted Lids

We sit down for lunch at the small table near the window, a wide bay window that stretches from ceiling to floor. I like the vista it offers, of the street just outside Shahana's house, people rushing by, so close that you can see the tops of their heads, the bags slung across their shoulders, the umbrellas they hold afloat, like signals. They don't see us though. I am facing the window, Shahana is opposite me, blocking some of the view. Where are they all going? I wonder idly.

This widening view, the sky stretching grey outside, is the only thing I like about her flat. The inside is so messy, I am having trouble remaining polite. However, I mustn't cringe, really I shouldn't. I need to continue eating since Shahana has asked me twice, 'Nita, is everything all right? Hope you like it?' She has served low fat food, in keeping with the diet she is on. Lean turkey mince in roasted peppers. Chicken salad with no mayo. I gulp water to swallow, not that I am a fussy eater, but this is so dry! Why has she invited me for lunch when she's on a diet? Is she wanting to show off that she can cook or that she has lost weight?

'You are lucky. You don't need to diet. You are so skinny,' she says. And indeed, I am, I don't need to diet, simply because I don't overeat. Everything in moderation.

Shahana eats heartily. I see the food lick her teeth, she talks, she always talks, incessantly. The lives of most of the women I know stretches infinitely over the mundane. How they can't stop eating chocolate, how they need to diet, how they need to go to the gym, how they need to clean wine glasses until they shine spotless, how the wash needs to be done with perfection, colour protect capsules for the coloured, whitening capsules with bleach for the whites.

'It's a bit dry, I know,' she continues. Turkey fibre on her left canine. I chew with my mouth closed. The only thing I like are the peppers.

'Should I have done the peppers a little more?' she asks.

'No, they are really fresh. Nice.'

'I got them from the market,' she beams. I listen attentively as she describes her visits to the farmers' market every Thursday. How it has been her routine for years.

That's the problem with my friends, they pick up these finer nuances of life from me but they don't admit it. Wasn't it at the last coffee morning that I'd mentioned I buy my kale from the farmers' market and never get the bagged ones from Waitrose? That the quail eggs are the best, and you can get quinoa in a large bag, from the shop at the end of the road. They copy liberally from my lifestyle and views, without ever attributing it to me. I have known this for long yet suddenly I feel my face flush, I feel this frisson of anger shoot across in my body, in my arms, flash across my chest.

'It's really bad, isn't it?' she asks, chomping all the time. I almost say yes, but my politeness takes over. Shahana and I went to college together, years ago. She has recently moved back from the Midlands, and she wants to meet often, have our children be friends. She wants to be like we were at college, our lives so like each other's.

'Not at all, it isn't. Don't worry.'

She wants to talk, really talk, heart-to-heart, woman to woman; how her husband is so busy that he returns late every day, how he doesn't help with the housework, how her son and daughter fight all the time.

'What about your two? Don't they fight?'

Actually, they don't. My two get along very well. Like Shahana's kids, Dylan and Tarah are also two years apart, yet they get on well.

'Yes, it's normal. They will squabble. Kids are like that,' I say.

'I worry sometimes, you know.'

'They will grow out of it,' I console. I do think her children quarrel a little too much but it's not easy to say such things.

The small flat closes on me, cloying colours of a golden-framed mirror on a purple highlighted wall, red flowers on cream curtains. The kitchen opens to the dining area, and from where I sit, I can see the pots and serving spoons in a heap, on the counter. It makes me want to be in my kitchen. The smell of fresh oranges. The huge vase of lilies on the counter. The hob polished and clean. The floor gleaming. I have tidied and wiped to sparkling-glass perfection this morning. I've also attended my morning yoga class, and on the way back stopped at the shops to buy myself a shift dress in navy blue crochet. Shahana says she has wasted most of her morning on Facebook and WhatsApp.

Lunch over, we take our plates into the kitchen and Shahana busies herself trying to serve dessert. 'I am very full,' I say. But she has made this special ice-cream cake a couple of days ago, so I must try it, really. I can take it home. She cuts a generous portion. 'Let me find a box to pack this in. Then Dylan and Tarah can have some as well.' She opens drawer after drawer, tries to fit lids on boxes, a few things rattle to the floor. 'Oh, sorry,' she says. 'I hate doing this sort of thing... wait, let me try something else.' I think of the cupboard in my kitchen, boxes stacked in threes, fitted lids. It irks me that she can't do something as simple as find a lid which fits a box.

She pulls out a tube of cling film from somewhere under the sink, and proceeds to tear it, but she doesn't hold it straight over the serrated edge like you should. The plastic rolls over and she loses the free end. She tries to rip it across. 'That should do. Let me get you a carrier bag.'

'Maybe I shouldn't. I need to run some errands. It will melt by the time I get home...' I am lying. The children have an after-school charity event – a pizza and movie evening. I am to pick them only at half past seven. I have no other plans for the afternoon; a cup of tea, do some of the ironing, make myself some dinner. 'It's all nicely sealed now. It will be fine, even if you do go the shops.' I watch her trying to flip the cling film over the Chinese takeaway plastic box. A few bubbles of chocolatey liquid brim around the box. Potato skins curl on the floor near the bin, grains of rice strewn on the floor where she hasn't hoovered. She could

130

have cleaned the place before asking me to come over for lunch or suggested we meet outside! We could have had lunch in the Café Rouge on the High Street, ordered some decent camembert but she said she had to do the diet.

Finally, the ice-cream cake is packed, and the box placed in a flimsy Tesco bag. At last, I can say my goodbyes. Shahana says, 'Coffee next week? I can come to yours.'

Out in the open the fresh air is redeeming, it strokes my face gently. I feel sick. I wish I hadn't eaten. The little flat with its messy kitchen was depressing. I tell myself it's unfair to compare. After all, I have a brand-new kitchen, Frank's gift on my birthday. It took the builders two months to put it in, and it's so worth it. My old kitchen wasn't this messy ever, I could offer Shahana tips to organise it but I don't think she would appreciate it. She knows I don't work now, but she still sees me as the career woman, the one who worked those long hours in the city.

Habituated to sitting at a desk, rushing for meetings, producing reports on time, travelling all over the world to meet clients. It's inbred in me. After Dylan, I had gone back to work for a bit but Tarah came quickly after. The pace of my new life was relaxing, so quaint in a way. The toddler groups I took my two to, the coffees and lunches with other mums, the walks in the park, pushing our prams along. I never went back to my job but life is busy. Frank often tells me to relax. He'd insisted we get a cleaner, and we had, but I never slacked off. Now that the children are older, and will soon be in secondary school, I have more free time, and several friends to fill it.

Ruhia from the mums' coffee morning group messages saying they are planning to go to town next week to visit the Ideal Home Show in Earl's Court. She will set up a WhatsApp group to plan the day. Was I interested? I agree. I do like the Ideal Home Show.

I drive home; it's only fifteen minutes from Shahana's house in Bromley to mine in Chislehurst. I am feeling unusually restless, I turn up the radio, I go a little faster than I usually would. Frank is back from Munich, only on Friday evening. He travels almost every week for work. My afternoon will spread out quietly over the kitchen, the oven, the ironing board, the still plants in the house. It's as if my brain cells are atrophying. I must go out, see something, do something different. I can't wait for a whole week for our little outing.

I think of my lunch time visits to the Tate Modern, when I used to work near the Borough Market. Shahana, Ruhia, Zoe, Jane, have never been there. It's not something they can think of, whiling time looking at these sculptures and paintings, some of it so strange, questioning your very essence. I haven't been there in years. I reach home, and as I walk in, I am planning instead. What if I drive to the station right now, take the next train to Waterloo? I could be there in twenty minutes, spend a couple of hours in the Tate, and be back by six in the evening, giving myself enough time to pick the kids up from school? The thought solidifies; I haven't done something like this in years, will it be too rushed? But it's only 1.30 p.m. and I pace it in my head. I can. I want to do it, right now. I quickly put Shahana's box in the fridge, grab a bottle of water, and rush back out. 'Skinny decaf latte,' my voice still has the same cadence as it did years ago, when I buy a coffee from the little shop at the station. The carriage is not very busy at this hour in the afternoon, but at Waterloo, it doesn't feel the same. I don't find any signs for the Tate Modern and I can't figure which is the best exit to take. And then the people! So many people, coming in from all directions, up the escalators, up the stairs, they come through the wide-open doors. They come in with books, buds stuck into ears, lost in music. I count four different ethnicities in one group. A young man comes in with a little dog. The dog wears a little coat, a chill setting in the autumn air. I am smiling at the dog, without thinking, then tell myself you don't smile at dogs, they won't know.

'You OK?' the young man says. He is looking concerned as if I am someone who needs looking after.

'I am fine, thank you,' I reply. I am sure I can find my way around. He nods and walks away. I think swiftly, I should try to get to the Southbank exit, walk along the river and cross over to the Tate.

I continue staring at the exits. It is so noisy with constant announcements – trains to Portsmouth and Bracknell and Poole and wherever not. I must get out of the station, so I purposely walk out through the first exit I see. I flick my Google maps and type in Tate Modern. That's when I realise

I was meant to walk towards Southwark from Waterloo East station and not towards Waterloo Mainline like I have done. I have got it wrong, the journey I had done for five years, suddenly unknown. I follow Google Maps on my phone. It's farther than I expect, and my wedge boots seem surprisingly uncomfortable.

Finally, I see the familiar outline of the Tate Modern. I want to first visit the room I used to like, with all the portraits in block prints. My feet used to know their way around here, but now it feels a foreign country, with stranger streets. I walk around, right, left, into a room, out of another, trying to look relaxed. I have worn a fitted striped jacket over my skinny jeans, to not look entirely casual. But the room is stuffy, I feel hot. I take it off and it adds to the weight of my Louis Vuitton tote. I want the Tate to shock, question, enrapture me, like it used to, but everything looks unknown.

On level 1, I go to Room 1 and find large canvases of various colours in various shapes hanging on the walls. I don't understand, I walk into Room 2. More colours, what emotions do the colours rouse in you? they ask. I know about colours. I had the walls of my kitchen painted lily white. I know it is calming. But I don't comprehend this room, a yellow shaped triangle hangs in the centre. What emotion is it meant to inspire? In another room a show called Blue is running, seventy-nine minutes I am told when I ask. I go upstairs instead, and walk through the museum, room after room. Odd shaped sculptures, strange paintings. My feet hurt, I think of the work I had planned to do. I find myself in front of Picasso's nude woman with a necklace. Her curves seem imperfect, how was it I had never noticed that before? I used to love this one.

'Nice but how can they compare it with the Mona Lisa?' someone says, and I notice the young woman to my right. She's wearing ripped denims and a cropped white top. A long-beaded necklace. I shrug my shoulders and say, 'Unique though.'

'Oh yes, of course... but the imperfection makes the perfection?'

I am not sure if she is talking to me or herself. I assume she is some sort of an art student.

'She was his wife, isn't it? To paint your wife this way...' I say looking at the nude woman's spread out thick legs, her eyes almost cross-eyed.

'Interesting,' she says. She gives a toothy smile and adds, 'It's so nice here, lovely to kill some time when the kids are at school.'

'You have kids at school?' I ask.

'Yeah, three! I drop them off and come here sometimes, just for a few hours. Good to get away, you know?'

'Indeed. I work close by. I come here for a short break sometimes.'

'That's nice! Lucky,' she looks impressed. I don't know why I said I worked, instead of mentioning my kids.

'I must rush now,' I say looking at my watch and pull out my phone to check for messages. 'See you.'

'So must I,' she trills, looking so much at home. I can't do this any longer. I want to be back in my house. I had planned to have a nice quiet dinner by myself, but it's getting late so I grab a salad from Pret, and eat it on the train, like the young girl sitting opposite me, and while she does it effortlessly, it feels unnatural to me.

I walk down the station path, towards my car, parked on Princess Avenue, one of those side streets with free parking. It's not the second left as I thought it would be. I walk on and arrive at the third left turn, which turns out to be Maple close. Soon there is a fourth bend, no sign of Princess Avenue still. I have come down the wrong road. I walk back to the station square. This is ridiculous. This is where I have lived since years, how can this be? I have never been lost before. I am not able to connect to Google maps for some reason. I am embarrassed but I ask an old gentleman, who looks like he knows the area. He smiles, 'Look, go down this road, you see where the car is coming out of?'

'That's the one isn't it?' I ask and laugh, as if I always knew. But once again I am back on the road with all the left bends and it's not the right road. Suddenly, the sun seems muted, and the sky darkens, evening is setting in. I am trembling. I must leave soon, to pick the kids up, so I must find the car soon. It's almost a thirty-minute drive to their school. I have never been late.

I ask another woman walking towards me, 'Excuse me,

where's Princess Avenue, do you know?' My voice has a catch in it. She looks around, as if hoping the road will appear suddenly. I do that sometimes when people ask me for directions, and I have no clue. She says, 'I have heard the name, but hmm let me think...,' eventually she gives up and shrugs, 'Why don't you ask the doctor's surgery, right there?' I say, 'OK thank you.' My hair is dishevelled. I feel the strands flying, thin, fine hair.

I go into the surgery. My voice is cracked; I try to hide the desperation. I live in this neighbourhood. I have been living here for ten years. Everything looks the same! The woman at the reception doesn't know, so she asks the other woman behind her. She looks at me as I ramble, 'You know I parked my car on that road this afternoon. Now I can't find it, isn't it silly. I just can't find it.' I laugh, to my ears even it sounds crazed.

'There dear, it's right there,' the lady comes outside with me, and points to a road round the bend. And then I see it, the familiar sign, Princess Avenue, the name of the road in its familiar font, I run to my car.

I reach home in ten minutes, my quiet perfect home. Through the wide hallway, into my kitchen. The water feature on the wall tinkles gently, slate grey. The waxy petalled orchids, white, pale pink, on the spotless island. The wind chime on the window tinkles gently in a breeze I can't feel. Perfection that I have built, beauty I have envisioned, my hard work, and yet, sameness, familiarity just like the houses next to mine.

I need a drink and open the fridge for a juice. The plastic box with the ice-cream cake from Shahana is sitting in the middle of the shelf. Streaks of chocolate all along the side of the box, drops under the lid, and a big blob splatters on the shelf. I let go of the fridge door and it slams shut. I sit on the plush bar stool, elegant cream. I think of how the city felt a stranger, how I got lost in the streets I know so well. The houses next to me, so like mine. The lives around, like mine, even if I think they aren't. Sameness. Routines fitting people perfectly like lids on boxes.

And then I scream. Suddenly. Loudly. The orange oriental lilies look placid in their wide vase. I reach out and strike it so the vase shatters on the floor. Shiny shards on the warm tiles, the water trickling through, the flowers fan out, the sticky pollen falls out.

I scream and scream. My kitchen stands mute.

Lovers in a Room

Once inside the room, the doors shut, the do not disturb sign hangs on the knocker, the lovers do what lovers are meant to. It's like the movies. They gaze at each other, smiles wider than American roads, reach out, fall into a hug, and their lips meet. A palm here, fingers impatiently pushing fabric away, gradually pushing onto the bed.

'You are an impatient kisser,' the man says.

'Really? No one has ever said this. Everyone says I kiss well,' All the twenty-one men she has kissed, and sometimes counts off her fingers on nights she can't sleep, spelling their names and the time she has spent with each in minutes. Everyone has loved her lips, the curve, the fullness.

It adds to the annoyance she felt when she met the man downstairs in the hotel lobby ten minutes ago and his first words were, 'Hey, I thought you would be taller.' And just like that, once again she was a schoolgirl, the shortest, the thinnest, the flattest girl in class. She had been the girl no boy had looked at, the one who didn't look up at anyone, face buried in her book.

He had added. 'You look so nice,' but it was too late, and that first sentence rose to the surface like oil droplets on water, and stayed.

'I need you, I must see you,' he had said often, his voice heavy with longing like tropical rain clouds. The man she had hoped could be the one; this man she met on a

Facebook group, and been chatting for months, about life, philosophy, love, poetry, especially the poetry. His voice, slightly rasping as if jagged edges of a gentle moon. So she has routed her travel from London to arrive a day early in Mumbai. Her meeting is in Bangalore tomorrow and she must fly by six in the morning to arrive on time.

He says her name now, thrice, in long, slow whispers, he shivers in her arms, as if he feels more than he can say. Slowly the clothes are off, but when he's inside her, she doesn't feel him. He pumps up and down, pounding, sweat droplets on his head, and she feels nothing. Her attention drifts, to the other men she has been with, how some can fill so completely, and some fill you with emptiness. How the one she had the best sex with lying across the corner of the bed was someone she didn't even like that much. The other man she meets in London at times, such a nice, gentle person, his bald head, patient between her legs, up and down like a giant egg. The egg-man is burly, his hairy torso fits on muscular legs, and she feels repulsed, yet comes in long shudders when she's with him.

In the hotel room now, even as her body contorts, and the man whispers her name and says, 'We came together.' Somewhere, a saddened part of her, weeps silently.
Her friend is to arrive shortly for a coffee.

'Did you have to meet her? It takes away time, from us,' the man says.

'I can't be in Mumbai and not meet her, she's an old friend!'

She goes downstairs when her friend calls.

Alone, the man busies himself making a joint. She has never smoked up and he finds this surprising. The girl of his dreams is someone he can have a joint with, has long, straight hair and large eyes. Beautiful breasts he can fondle, fall into, rest on, a refuge. This woman feels inadequate. He hadn't expected her to be so tiny, so small. He had seen her on video calls, and she'd seemed curvy. He had longed to meet her. But he wishes they could have met somewhere else, a beach resort, a retreat in the mountains, somewhere open, outdoors. He feels trapped in the room, his anxiety surges. She could only spare a day between her international travel, and this was the only option she provided. She is some sort of a corporate hotshot.

He still misses the one before, the one he loved so much that he went crazy when she left him. He was prescribed medication for months. Those wide eyes, the large breasts, the alabaster skin. He can still taste the sweat between her breasts, feel her heavy, dense body on his. He continues to powder the leaves; smokes another cigarette.

She sits by the pool with her friend, talk as if they are back in school, two young girls in plaits, about common friends and who is where, doing what. The sun sets, like it does in the tropics, abruptly. The woman looks up at the moon, which has appeared, a bright Venus close to it, like a lover, she thinks. She doesn't say she has a man in the room upstairs. Doesn't mention the planning she's had to do to meet the man, spend a day with him, leaving behind the children and her husband – estranged husband. It has been a few months since they agreed to separate, yet they are waiting, as if someone else will instruct, 'You must now leave the ship, it is sinking in any case.' They are carrying on, married, knowing that they are separate, as if parallel stretches of roads. Once the divorce is agreed, she will be legally single. Free. She knows about her husband's affairs too. She doesn't mention any of this to her friend, when she enquires about the family. Instead, she makes an excuse that she has work to finish, a dinner to go to.

Back in the room, she makes the man some tea, and he takes the proffered cup without thanks, as if he expected it, and she imagines his mum serving him. He lives with his parents. Single and thirty-six. She doesn't ask about his past loves, she imagines he has found and lost. She feels he has pined and suffered, and some part of her wants to heal him.

'Let's go downstairs to smoke up,' he says.

She is wearing a silk cami and her ripped jeans. I will kiss your honeyed thighs wherever there is a rip, he had said when she'd sent a photo before, but now, nothing, not a word.

'Bring me some jasmine,' she had asked.

'Jasmine?'

'Love the Indian jasmine, petalled clusters!'

'Let me see what I can do.'

But he arrived with nothing. 'No jasmine. There were roses though.'

And you didn't bring me one? She wanted to say but didn't. Her words are trapped as if fireflies in a jar.

Back at the empty pool, the fading stars; city smog perhaps, when she had expected a glittering sky. Some birds take flight, a strain of an old song from somewhere, a sharp twinge; she misses her home, her children even though both are in their teens, hardly dependent on her anymore. She thinks of the others she could have met today. She feels alone. The man is next to her, blowing smoke rings.

They wander to the room; he is hungry. They order room service. He doesn't offer to pay for any of his meals. He opens one of the wines she has brought, with a male swagger. She tells herself she mustn't think traditionally, expecting the man to pay, to look after her. She, a modern woman, who earns six figures, surely she mustn't resent this little man's–. She bites her lips as she realises she has thought *little man*. Even in her mind, she doesn't want to belittle him, wants to give him a chance. Yet when they are on the bed again, the lights are on, and he sips the cold white wine and then kisses her, lets it drip on her chest, and licks the drops off her, yet, and yet, her thoughts drift again.

'What's the perfume?' he asks.

'Ma Vie. Do you like it?' It's her favourite.

He doesn't know. 'A bit strong,' is all he says.

Love making over, the man sits on the single sofa. When she comes up and wants to sit close to him, on him, he starts, 'I am sitting here,' he points to the footrest in front. 'You can sit there.' Something snaps in her like china breaking on her kitchen floor, on one of the fights with the husband. It annoys her so much she walks to the desk, opens up her laptop, and starts responding to work emails. He sits as if paralysed, not realising anything, something is wrong.

The food arrives, breaking the silence. Spicy potato wedges, crisp on the outside, soft on the inside. Pomfret grilled to perfection. He removes the bone, and places forks of fish in her mouth. They finish another bottle of wine. The music plays on her Spotify, she can't place the songs, but the music is wild, it uplifts her. And she kisses him, when he is standing. Surprised. He responds. He holds her, strokes her arm. Kisses her neck. Once again on the bed. 'Suck my toes,' he says. And she does. They make love until the wine finishes, the music runs over and over. The room smells of smoke. Non-smoking room, yet he has been smoking.

She wants to sleep, the jetlag catching up with her. She wants to sleep with someone who can really touch her, complete her. She thinks of other men, the estranged husband. How in the early days, they would wake in the morning and kiss, when the sun came in through the thick curtains, shadows and ripples on their bodies, how nothing else mattered, how they could have spent all morning in bed, not thinking about the office. Those days, she used to believe, this was it, they would always be like this, together.

144

But it changed, he changed, she changed, nothing is the same.

She is almost asleep. The man asks if she wants dinner.

'It's past midnight,' she says.

'I am hungry. May be room service?'

'Let's go downstairs, to the twenty-four hours dining.' She can't bear food smells in a room she wants to sleep in, and she doesn't like plates stacked outside the room, food drying in streaks.

He loves his food, she can see. He orders khichdi, and it comes steaming, rice cooked with vegetables, all in a mush, and the smell of the spice makes her hungry. He shares some. On the way back to the room he holds her hand. As if they are together. A couple, anyone would assume.

It is almost two. The lovers know they must sleep now. He sleeps silently. Not like the husband who snored so much, tossed so much, night after night, she curled up, first with one child, and then the other, then in the spare room. Sometimes on the sofa like a cat. Sometimes in the study with the books. One night she slept in the utility room, wrapped in an old duvet, freshly smelling clothes laundered around her.

Her alarm goes, it's four a.m. She reaches out to shut it, but, the man grasps her arm. He is fast asleep but he holds on to her hand, an iron grip, 'Let go honey,' she says and uses her left hand, to pull the right out, reaches over and stops the alarm.

Showered, dressed in a white shirt and red trousers, she

bends and kisses him, he pulls her closer. 'You've already showered? You look lovely,' and she is on him and once again he tries, he pulls on a condom. He goes soft, pounding inside her, and she feels nothing. She is impatient now.

'I must go, it will get late.'

He helps with her case. She checks out and tells reception her friend will stay in and give the keys back. They are strict about security, they note his name, they check if she paid for a double room. Outside, he kisses her again, she responds with a quick one on the cheek. She doesn't think she will ever meet him again. As the taxi moves, he waves.

Back in the room, the man tries to fall asleep. He doesn't understand why he couldn't perform. He should have had his anxiety medication before, he was so nervous. He hasn't been with a woman for months, has he developed some problem? Besides, he had expected her to be more talkative, she hardly said anything or asked him about his life. He had wanted to describe, how the love of his life had left him, how his parents want him to have an arranged marriage, how he wants to find someone he really loves. He doesn't like using condoms but she had been adamant, and that added to his nervousness. She seemed too practical for someone as sensitive as him. He nestles into the pillow, everything smells a little of her, a fresh shower smell and the perfume he had liked, strong though it was. He tries to forget the moment she asked, 'Oh are you really inside, couldn't make out.' He has never done the wine thing with anyone before, and with the thought of it, he feels himself going hard. Surely she liked him a lot? He wonders what he will do if she insists on meeting him again. He is not sure if he wants to, but as his hand moves faster and faster on his penis, now upright, he thinks why not. He will meet her again. He falls asleep, and wakes mid-morning. Before he checks out, he stands at the window, takes a photo of the outside, some buildings, a bit of the sky. He sends it to her.

She messages back, what is this?

Don't you recognise it? It's the view from the window. He had thought she would like it as a memory of the day. He says his backpack is full of the gifts she brought him. He is in a haze. Why? she asks. And he says, from the lovemaking. She responds her day is busy and she plans to go out, meet a friend in the evening.

She has brought nothing back from the man. She feels emptier than before.

After her meeting she will go to her hotel. She will change into a blue dress and go out to meet another friend. They will go to a rooftop bar and talk all evening. When the rain clouds arrive, they will leave, he will drive her to the hotel, and somewhere on that journey, they will turn breathless, kissing, hands hungry on each other. She will try and complete herself a little more, add a thought, an experience, and hope it will be better than the last time.

Another room, another man.

Why does the Cricket Sing?

Silence sat in the Biology class, heavy, unmoving like the buffaloes outside Rose's house in the small town of Berhampur. A deep silence. A silence unusual for thirteen-year olds. Rose watched the sun's rays, slant through the sky-lights, and diffuse in the room, she could feel the pin-drop silence, as ordered by Miss Indira, in her very bones.

Rays of the sun slanted through the sky-lights in her classroom, that Rose found she could hear things she hadn't before: the steady hum of the ceiling fan, a faint rustle as someone in the front row turned a page, a catch in the breath as someone tried to supress a giggle, a ttrr ttrr as a cricket sang low on the windowsill. The rasping whisper of Miss Indira sliced through the air into her skin. That whisper would lie low in Rose's blood for years, and like a hooded cobra rise to deride her.

'You two are dangerous. Vulgar. At this age!' Miss Indira said and laughed a loud laugh that shattered the silence and encouraged the children to join in. Judge and jury and witnesses. She was perched on the desk, commanding, raven-like. Her thin chiffon saree had slipped, and right there, at the top of her black blouse, a deep cleavage was visible. The word cleavage slotted itself into Rose's mind only when she was older; at that moment, she had looked on, not able to tear her eyes away. When Miss Indira leaned forward, her black saree slid down a bit more, the left and right breasts pushed against each other like the class twins Raju and Sanju when they queued up for assembly.

Years later – aged fifteen, sixteen, and even twenty – Rose would look back upon that day; at her just-turned-thirteen-year old self, standing next to her best friend Seema, and shiver.

Two small girls caught as if deer before headlights. She, an inch shorter than Seema, flat like a roti. The only girl so flat, so out of curiosity, she had developed a habit of looking out for the faint outline of bra straps under the girls' white school-uniform-shirts, imagining little chests plumping up, hard buds forming behind white bras, and worrying when her own breasts would grow.

'Do you hear that sound?' Miss Indira continued, 'It's a cricket. These insects seem active all day in our school grounds, in fact this ttrr ttrr is even louder at dusk. And do you know why they make that noise? It's the male trying to attract the female. Not the female, the male! If the females did it, it would be abnormal. Vulgar! Even in the animal world. And you! At this age to think of love. Do you realise what you girls have done?!'

What had they done? Rose didn't know, she looked at Seema, but Seema was staring ahead steadfastly. Seema, her best friend since they were seven, wore her *I will not talk about it* expression. Just like the time she had borrowed Anna's copy of *Five on a Treasure Island* and spilled water on it, so the pages stuck to each other, and wouldn't confess. Her face stiff, closed.

Miss Indira turned to the boys. 'Raj and Hiren, can you stand up please?'

Raj, small, skinny. Hiren, much taller, handsome even at this age, and with the knowledge he was handsome, at this age.

'So what do you have to say about this err... incident?'

Raj looked downcast and said nothing.

Hiren looked up. 'Miss Indira, I am really upset about this unfortunate incident. My father has been transferred to Rotarpur, and we are moving soon. I will join the best school there. If anyone hears of this in my new school it will spoil my reputation.' Hiren enunciated well. In the debate competitions at school, he usually won a prize, mostly in second place since Rose was almost always first.

'What do you have to say, Rose?'

'About what? I don't know what you mean.'

'Don't you, Rose? You seem to be the main character in this story.'

'No, Miss. I don't,' and she didn't. Though she had heard titters when she walked into the classroom yesterday. In the break, she had noticed Rita and Sumi whisper to each other, glance at her, and stop when she caught their eye.

'Anything wrong, Sumi?' she'd asked as boldly as she could.

'You'll soon find out.' Sumi had broken into giggles.

'What will I find out?' she asked but the girls walked away.

Miss Indira continued, 'And you Seema, do you know

what this is about?'

Seema was silent, her face still frozen, a slab of ice.

'Would anyone like to explain?' Miss Indira's gaze swept across the room, telescope-like. Someone lifted their hand up.

At twenty, Rose couldn't remember who it had been, just that it was a boy from the last row, wearing a yellow house badge, the face blurred in her memory. The voice was quiet, as if in shock, as if the speaker had seen something he had never expected.

'Miss, these things have been going on here for a while. It is not nice. We feel we are not old enough for such things…'

'What things?' a stage whisper.

'Well, love…and they wanted to do more… they spoke of…'

'Speak louder!'

'K-k-kissing...'

A gasp across the room as if a tornado ripped through.

'Even more…doing more…touching…'

'What are you talking about?' Rose asked, suddenly angry. Everyone knew except her. Everyone was trying to make her feel she had committed some mistake but what? And why?

Rita stood up. 'I was the one who found the note.'

'Who had written it?' Miss Indira interrupted.

'It was signed by Rose'

'Pass the note around. Let us all see it.'

It reached Rose a scrunched-up ball. The handwriting almost indecipherable, written in block letters:

I LOVE HIREN AND I WANT TO KISS HIM!
I WANT HIM TO TOUCH ME.
I KNOW YOU LOVE RAJ.
HAVE YOU TOLD HIM YET?
Rose

At first glance, it looked like her handwriting, but it couldn't be, since she hadn't written it! How had they copied her signature but before she could scrutinise it, the voice commanded, 'Pass it on.'

Eager hands reached out and accusing eyes read the note. 'I really don't like this, Miss. I don't want my parents to know.' Hiren said, all red in the face, as if embarrassed.

Rose turned and tried to catch his eye, but he was looking ahead at Miss Indira. Last week, she had won the inter-school elocution competition. Hiren was placed third and an older girl from the All Girls Govt School was in the second position. He hadn't congratulated Rose.

Hiren and Rose. Rose and Hiren. Friends, competitors. Only she was good enough for him. Only he was good enough for her. The comics they exchanged, 'one for one' to be returned in two days. The Enid Blyton books they bought from the little bookstore in town. The most avid readers in the class. They spoke perfect English, got lead roles in the school play, no one else could come close. Every Holi, Seema invited her over, then Hiren would arrive with his friends. A boisterous coloured-water fight would ensue, the girls hiding in the balcony and chucking water balloons at the boys outside. At lunchbreak, Seema and Rose day-dreamed, futures in university, the four of them, Hiren for Rose, Raj for Seema. They never mentioned it to the boys, but didn't everyone in the class acknowledge this special friendship? Just like in the movies.

Aged twenty-five, Rose would still remember how Biology wasn't taught that day. Instead Miss Indira had spoken about how young girls needed to be careful. How easy it was to be misled, do things you were not meant to, and get into trouble.

'So should they be punished?' Miss Indira asked the class. 'They need to realise this is wrong.'

Forty-one young heads nodded, 'Yes Miss.' Only Rose stayed silent.

'Focus on your studies. Don't waste your parent's money. Bad characters fall in love. Do not touch each other until you are married. Remember this!'

Miss Indira wasn't married. There were whispered stories about her and the Maths teacher Mr. Rao, who was married and had three children. A couple of years ago, Mrs. Rao had come to the school, stormed into the staff room and flung someone's cup of hot tea on Miss Indira's arm. A screaming Miss Indira, blisters erupting on her skin, had been rushed to the dispensary. Now, Miss Indira's left arm stayed covered by her unpinned saree, her long hair hung in a plait down her back, and dark circles expanded under her eyes as if she never slept. Rose counted the spots on Miss Indira's face, three dark moles on the left cheek, large pock marks on the right, while she continued, 'And you boys, you should be careful about girls like these. You should know when to stop talking to them and reach out to your teachers and parents to warn us of such bad behaviour.'

It was the best school in town; co-educational, English-medium, run by Christian missionaries, who tried to get everyone to speak English the way they did in England. The nuns, called sisters, usually from Kerala, lived inside the school complex, in the mysterious boarding area the children were curious about but were not allowed into. They wore white habits, their hair covered, their tunics fitted to the waist, then pleated down to their ankles. Then there were the local teachers, dressed in sarees, who lived in the older part of town with the narrow streets. A few spoke fluent English the way they were supposed to but most spoke in local accents no one wanted to own. The sisters preached that girls and boys were equal. Girls are just as clever and as good as boys. No discrimination, they instructed. They advised in the assemblies, in the parents-teachers' meetings. They spoke to the parents who produced daughter after daughter, all conceived in the hope of a boy. Rose, and her younger sister Lilly, were often held up as perfect examples, two girls and see how clever and talented they are. See how proud their parents are.

Miss Indira continued, 'Do you know what happens when you get into this love stuff when you are young, and before you are married? Have you seen those fruits of sin? The babies left outside the orphanage?'

A collective breath sprinted across the class.

An orphanage stood right next to the school. Sometimes little babies were left on the steps, wrapped in old soft sheets; if boys, wrapped loosely, proudly, so that the gender was established quickly. Girls were well covered, their little legs and their in-betweens swathed tightly. The hope was that the baby would be taken in, and only later they would realise it was a girl. Unfounded fears, since the sisters insisted that every baby girl would be looked after.

'If you want to kiss at twelve, thirteen, you have to be careful that you don't lose your virginity at fifteen. Then you will shame yourself and your family.'

The class sniggered, words such as virginity never uttered so openly. The class clown Manoj laughed loudly.

Miss Indira turned to him, 'Yes, you should laugh. This is how we can stop such problems in our society. Laugh at them so they do not repeat. Be cruel to be kind. To imagine girls doing this! I am ashamed of you, Rose and Seema, especially you Rose. All those prizes and certificates, of no use. And…,' here a long pause, 'Well, I know your community doesn't have the same values. You Anglo-Indians, bit too modern for us, aren't you? But for girls to have no morals at this age! Is this what your parents teach you? Is this what Christian values teach you?'

Miss Indira explained the rules of good behaviour for girls. How they should walk in public with their heads down in public, how they should never talk to strange men, how they shouldn't fall in love before getting married, and how they should safeguard their virginity.

'Say sorry, the pair of you. Apologise to the class. This minute.'

'Sorry,' Seema said immediately. Quickly, simply.

'Good girl. I hope you have learnt your lesson. Your turn, Rose.'

'I haven't done anything wrong. Why should I say sorry?'

'You wrote a vulgar note. It's your handwriting.'

'I didn't write that note. Someone has tried to copy my handwriting.'

'Why would they?'

Yes, why would they? Who disliked her enough – Rita who had wanted to win the elocution contest and lost to her – Sumi who was Hiren's neighbour and wanted to exchange books with him, whereas he ignored her and offered Rose the first pick – Seema forced by them to speak untruths – or Hiren jealous that he had lost to her in the competition? Or Miss Indira who was known to be unkind to girls, especially the pretty and talented ones? All of them? It was only when she was much older, she understood there was one other reason she was singled out – the outsider, the only one not from the same community.

'I don't know. I am not in love with Hiren, and I don't

want to kiss him,' said Rose.

More gasps that she had uttered the word.

'You are really shameless, aren't you? Do you all think these girls have learnt their lesson? Or should we tell Sister Florian?'

Sister Florian knew her parents. They met at church. Surely she would question Rose and call her parents in. The shock on their faces – to think Rose, their pride would let them down like this! Lilly would be teased in school. Everyone would know, their aunts, uncles. And deep down, Rose worried about herself, how curious she had been when her older cousins described the kissing in the new movie *Dirty Dancing*. She had asked, 'How do they kiss? What about their noses, doesn't it get in the way?' That evening she had practised puckering in front of the mirror. She had imagined lips on hers, felt a tingling between her legs. Her fingers slipped deep inside her knickers, stroking, her thighs pressed against each other, and that pleasure was...

'So dangerous!' Miss Indira continued, her voice loud. 'Why don't we do something? Why don't I take you to Sister Florian, tell her the whole story, and let her come and talk to students of this class. Let her see what this so-called good student Rose Joseph is really like! Let her wonder what church teaches you!' Miss Indira continued, smirking openly.

'Sorry,' Rose mumbled.

'What was that?' Miss Indira asked, head cocked to one side, saree pulled up to decency.

'I am sorry. I didn't write the note, but sorry.'

'Well, well, that's a result. Even though you should admit you wrote it, since you did. I hope everyone has learnt something today. I hope you will all never make a mistake like this.'

The bell rang after a few minutes and Miss Indira walked out of the room, smiling, victorious. The next teacher came in, and everyone went back to their books. Rose didn't mention it at home. She waited for days in case a letter would arrive for her parents, she jumped every time the phone rang. For days after, she noticed the children looking at her and turning away, boys smirking and the girls hastily stopping their giggles when she arrived. Then school was out for the summer. Hiren left town. Rose and Seema never spoke again. Miss Indira didn't teach the senior classes, and Rose averted her eyes if she ever saw her in the school corridors. She worked even harder, did even better in her lessons. She went to graduate college in Mumbai, then moved to Paris for a postgraduate. The farther, she went, the happier she felt.

But some things remained. A hiss rose in her blood and shouted, *vulgar! dangerous!* when she responded to a boy's lips, her body wanting more. Sometimes, especially when desire tempted her to forget herself, forget the boundary of her limbs and melt, want, need, devour the man she was with, fuck to eternity; she would stop, shrink away, and then ignore them.

When the Italian boy she'd kissed twice wanted more, she said she was travelling away for a month. He saw her in a café a few days later and shouted, 'You fucked up tease.' When the boy from India, with his curly hair and shining eyes, asked her out for dinner and invited her to his flat for the night for the second time, she said, 'I have a phobia of crickets. I think I can hear them in your flat.' He glared, shrugged his shoulders and said, 'You could have just said you don't like me, bitch!'

And then there was Antoine. She met him in the lifts at work. He in the office on the fourth floor and she on the sixth. Every day they smiled at each other, until one day they planned to meet for a coffee, then lunch, then dinner. One evening, when they were walking back together, an autumn warmth in the air, he asked if he could kiss her. They had known each other for two months. 'I don't want to,' she said, and watched the hurt grow in his soft brown eyes. But instead of calling her various names, he continued to meet her, again and again. He didn't force her. She tried to tell herself she wasn't thirteen anymore. She didn't have to listen to the rules. She ought to forget the rasping whisper in her blood. She gave in to him, slowly, gradually.

Yet, a whole year later, at twenty-seven, she shouted angrily, 'Aren't you ashamed?' when Antoine turned to her late in the night, his arms around her, kissing her ears. She squirmed.

'Ashamed?' he asked.

'Wasn't once enough?' she had invited him back to hers

that evening. Her miniscule flat in Montmartre from where they could see the city stretch out.

'Rose? I didn't get you?' his English halting, flaky, so beautiful.

'So stupid, embarrassing...'

'Let me love you...'

'You are disgusting.' She moved away.

'Why do you do this? Tell me... what is upsetting you?'

'I am like this. Dangerous. Why don't you get it?'

'Rose... Listen... why do you hurt me? Don't you know I–'

'Leave me alone!' She turned on her side and heard him sigh softly.

'Goodnight then.'

She had worried he might walk out, but he lay on his back, his arm stretched towards her, his fingers gently on hers. She watched him fall asleep, his breath getting heavy then settling like the steady hum of a river at peace, his ribcage rising gently under his light grey t-shirt. She interlaced her fingers in his and he didn't stir. Antoine who always waited for her with infinite patience like calm, still water, whose voice whispered like the rain, who wanted to visit India, meet her parents in Kerala. Antoine, who could surely kiss away that Friday afternoon, and all that it had touched and deformed in her life, if she let him. She tightened his arm over her, splaying his fingers on her breast. She thought all night, dissecting that day into scenes, into minutes, letting that rasping whisper dissolve, disappear.

She woke him later, hours later, when it was not yet dawn, but almost, when the clouds were pink outside. Curled up in the duvet, she could see the sky through a chink in the curtains. He looked at her puzzled, eyes sleep laden still. 'Listen,' she whispered, 'Do you know why the cricket sings?'

Formations

Rukmini wills herself to stay lying on the sofa. Om, Om Shanti, she chants. The ghosts dance, screaming in a frenzy, wild shapes tearing at her eyelids, at her mind. Voices calling out as if to say, 'Come with us. We have come from far. We will take you away. Come...' As if a great breeze has whipped into the living room and is tugging at her hair, her clothes, as if the cushions will start to float soon. She keeps her eyes shut. Calmness, Om, Om, Om. Slowly they disappear, the anger in the room passes. Outside it is still dark.

It is November. Rukmini wakes at four in the morning just like she did at home in India. Except here, in her daughter's home in England, the darkness lies deep and heavy. By the time the sun breaks through the greyness, and shines in its typical muted manner, Rukmini has done her pujas, showered, cooked the breakfast, and read a few pages of the Gita. Then Prasad wakes, and she makes some more tea. They like to drink endless cups of Earl Grey sitting on the flowered sofas in the conservatory, warmed by the electric heaters.

Today, she hesitantly tells Prasad about her experience.

'Once again? But how can you believe, even imagine, there are ghosts here?'

He points towards the houses on either side, the one on the left attached to theirs, the one on the right, a foot away, a dark brown fence between. Suburbia outside London, a place dotted with flowers and greenery. It's like holidaying in an Indian hill station.

'They are out there,' she points at the conifers at the bottom of the garden. The trees stand very tall making the house as private as a semi-detached can be. She has taken some time to understand the nuances; flats, terraced, townhouses, bungalows, semi-detached, detached houses.

'Don't mention this to Chaya. She won't be pleased,' he says.

'I have to. I want them out of here. They are creating havoc in our Chaya's life.'

Prasad is looking at Rukmini askance, his expression asks *are you joking?* but she looks serious. Over the past few days, she has been talking about the presence of evil spirits; ludicrous to think of ghosts in this calm oasis. He tries to stop his smile, but it is too late.

'You don't believe me, do you? I will tell Chaya to get those trees cut.' She is convinced there is a vibration, a negative formation in the house. That is the reason Chaya's life isn't blossoming the way it should.

They hear footsteps upstairs. The acoustics in this house surprised them at first, every footstep, every whisper amplified. It is Chaya. They are confident they can differentiate between their daughter's footsteps and their son-in-law's.

Chaya comes in and slumps on the sofa. Her hair is a mess, curly locks wound over each other, just like when she was a teenager.

Rukmini starts without any preamble, 'Why don't you get those trees cut down?'

'What trees?' she stares outside as if she has just registered the trees.

Rukmini knows Chaya doesn't want to discuss this immediately after waking. She has been very busy at work for the last month, often leaving early and returning late. Yet she continues, 'It would look so nice and tidy.'

'Oh. They give us some privacy,' Chaya says, her eyes narrowing, the way they do when she is feeling cross.

'But you would get more light in. You could grow vegetables, have a kitchen garden. It seems so eerie now.'

'Eerie?' Chaya gets up. 'I've left my phone upstairs.'

'What will you have for breakfast?' Rukmini calls out.

'Don't mind. Doesn't matter.' They hear her run up the wooden stairs.

Prasad sighs, 'Did you have to tell her now?'

'When am I supposed to have a proper chat with her?'

∞

It's almost ten when Chaya and Satyan emerge. Satyan says in a jovial way which Rukmini doesn't really appreciate.

'What are we having for breakfast? Puris?' He looks delighted at the stack of plump puris on the kitchen counter. She has made a light potato curry. The way he likes it.

Her son-in-law declares himself a foodie, and loves her cooking, unlike Chaya; she will just have cereal – not even

164

cornflakes with warm milk and sugar like she did as a child – but unsweetened muesli, sometimes a croissant and coffee. For lunch, even on weekends, she insists on a salad, cuts an avocado in half, chucks its round ball of a seed into the bin. The cold food her daughter eats surely can't be helping her.

After breakfast, when Rukmini is surveying the fridge to decide the menu for lunch – and thinks of making some fish cutlets, Chaya appears and says, 'Ma. It's come.'

'Don't worry, it will happen soon.' Rukmini wants to reach out and stroke her daughter's face, so delicate, fine-featured, to hug her slim body, which she takes to the gym every other day, but her daughter stands a foot away, her shoulders slumped.

Chaya laughs. Rukmini knows that laughter. The one Chaya launches into whenever she is lost, and it happens so often. Quick to despair, quick to lose hope, as if the grief was only hers to bear, as if no one else could understand.

'How long is soon? It has been a year and half already.'

'What does Satyan say?'

'He is fed up, Ma. He says if it has to happen it will but he can't take this stress anymore. He thinks I am being obsessive, and all this is adversely affecting his work.'

'Why don't you go to see another doctor?'

'He thinks we should give up.'

'Another doctor could help, maybe IVF?'

'But my gynaecologist is the best, don't you get it?' she stomps away again.

Prasad is blissfully watching something on the telly and smiling to himself. Rukmini comes up to him.

'She is upset. No luck this month also and Satyan isn't being supportive.'

'But the doctor says the tests are normal for both... and what is Satyan's issue now?'

'I told her to change the doctor.'

'You did not! You know she is upset. First the trees, now the doctor. How could you?!'

'Well, if you know what to say, why aren't you there to say it? I was only trying to help. Eighteen months and nothing. Surely the doctors should do something? Remember my friend Minati? Her daughter in America had IVF and had twin girls. She was thirty-eight! Chaya is a bit younger.'

'It will happen. Surely my daughter will not be so disappointed in life. God can't be so cruel.'

'I have already promised I will light a thousand diyas in the Jagannath temple, if she conceives soon.'

'How soon?'

'I don't know. You can't demand that way.'

She looks out of the kitchen window. In the daylight, now that the sun is higher in the sky, everything looks innocuous. Some autumn flowers, she doesn't know the names of, have bloomed, very colourful but with no fragrance. But she cannot forget the despair of the night, it had felt so solid. Something in the house which prevents anything good from happening. Something that isn't right.

She thinks for a while and decides she will do a puja to drive away the ghosts. She will cook Chaya meals with warming Ayurvedic ingredients, then her daughter will surely conceive. She needs to eat some food cooked with love, recipes from her childhood.

∞

On Monday, Chaya walks out of the house and walks ten minutes to the station. They moved here two years ago from the heart of London, like people do, when they want to start a family. The landscaped gardens, the parks, young parents pushing prams. The ambience can do nothing when nature isn't willing.

After a while, sex becomes just that, mere contortions in bed with no purpose, every month her period comes right on time like a trusted friend. Five days after the onset, the ovulation thermometer indicates she is at her most fertile. Sometimes she has to force Satyan.

'I have a headache tonight,' he complained. It struck her as ironic, a man using the age-old excuse of a woman. He went to bed, two painkillers later. In the morning, she reminded him, 'Still at the most fertile.' He turned over and dutifully pushed the liquid out of him.

'Something is wrong with the angle perhaps,' she had said, propping her bottom on pillows. She feels sticky drops on her thighs. 'I am not sure if anything is staying in.'

'That's the way it is, I think,' he said, getting up swiftly for a shower. No more soft kissing after they were done, no more lying across his chest, talking pasts and futures. The act had to be dutifully done twice a day to maximise chances. Except nothing worked.

Now she gets on her train, doing her make-up with swift strokes. She gets out at London Bridge, walks up Southwark Street, and through Borough market, past skinned rabbits and plump cupcakes, past purple kale and gutted seabass, up to the flat with its blue door. She knocks and he opens up in a flash.

'Right on time,' Ronan says.

The minute he shuts the door, she is in his arms.

'Hmm, you smell of toast,' she says. 'Warm toast.'

'And you smell delicious as always.'

'New perfume though!'

'Perfume takes the smell of skin. Did you know?'

On the couch, warm orange, they divest each other of everything they are wearing, a stone jumper, dark red trousers, blue jeans, grey t-shirt; all in a heap. She feels fierce, she feels needy, and Ronan knows her well, knows how to calm her body, her frantic mind and set her back into the day.

They leave together but in separate directions and he hands her a paper bag, her favourite almond croissant, he gets them from the little café Mabel's, down the road.

'I am so hungry, thank you.'

∞

The fridge is filled with tiny boxes with lids. Rukmini looks into one and finds some dried pasta shells stuck to each other, as if put into boiling water, but removed hastily.

'Why do you have all these little boxes of food?' she asks Chaya. 'Can I throw this?' She rattles the box.

'I thought I might use it when I make penne again.'

'But will you? Why not just throw it away before you forget it's there?'

'Don't like wasting food,' she says, walking away. It makes Rukmini smile. Why does Chaya worry about a minor wastage when they indulge extravagantly otherwise? The number of shoes Chaya owns is mind-boggling. The other day, they were in Oxford Street, and she walked into a large store, and within minutes was out, with a Topshop bag. A pair of shoes, some skinny jeans, a lace top.

Rukmini wishes her daughter could shop for baby clothes instead.

∞

Rukmini makes rich curries, she stirs cream into chicken, she steams fish, marinates it in mustard sauce then bakes in tender leaves, fries eggs in butter.

'Will Chaya eat any of that?' Prasad comments watching her labour in the kitchen.

'She has to. This will help, warm her insides. None of that cold angrez stuff she keeps having.'

Prasad laughs so loudly that she turns back to the simmering pot. In a restaurant, at lunch the other day, Chaya had ordered some moule-mariniere — mussels she explained to them – as if it was part of their daily diet. She scooped the tiny bit of flesh expertly, one mussel after the other, and Rukmini commented, 'How can a daughter of mine eat a bowl of seashells and like it?' they had all laughed.

For the spirits, she makes a special black ladoo. She rolls flour, sugar, purple food colouring, and folds the secret powder mixture of cinnamon, nutmeg, almonds, into small perfect balls. She will offer them every day in the puja, and then to Chaya and Satyan.

∞

The next day, Chaya leaves work early, and hurries to meet Ronan at the Rake, one of his favourite pubs. He works as a creative director in a production house and she feels his creativity touches everything he does. Once he bought oysters from the fishmonger, and showed her to how to slurp all the saltiness, aren't oysters the best aphrodisiac? she joked. He wants to cook tonight and stops for some fresh egg pasta on the way to the flat.

He likes cooking for her. He arranges salami, prosciutto, cheeses on a platter, cooks anchovies in olive oil, and grates courgettes into ribbons for her prawn linguine. He serves it on the round marble table by the bay window, as she lights candles.

'I can't stay for dinner. My parents will be waiting,' she says.

'Can I meet them?' He is smiling, his hands clasping hers.

'Wouldn't that be good?' she sighs, wondering what they

would say if she introduced him. Her mother, scandalised, her father, more patient. But their eyes would fill with shame. How could you, our son-in law is a gem, they would say.

'But why can't it be, Chaya? When will you tell them?'

'Don't start that again.'

'But we have to talk!'

'I thought that was meant to be the woman's dialogue.'

'It's not funny, Chaya. You need to decide.' He has stopped. He is looking at her, into her. His hands are on her waist.

'It wasn't meant to be serious when we started. You had a girlfriend, remember. Sarah, I think.'

'You know I am not using you.'

And she does. She knows how he feels for her.

Some months earlier, they met at a mutual friend's birthday in a crowded wine bar. Later they would try to deduce how they had ended up in the same cab going back to the friend's flat. Satyan had been away on one of his long work trips and she had stayed, like many of them, drinking into the next morning. Ronan and she exchanged numbers, though they hadn't met, until months later at the same friend's again. 'Nothing serious, just once,' she had said, when that night, very drunk, they had kissed out on the terrace. But they hadn't been able to stop. For a month now, Ronan has been saying, 'Leave him. We have to give ourselves time.'

'It's hard,' she says now. She has said this before.

'You don't love him, do you?'

'It's not about love.'

'What is it about then?'

'I want a baby.'

'Well, someday. But now…we need time together.'

'I am trying to have a baby, I mean.'

He is silent for a minute, then she sees comprehension in his eyes. Light-brown eyes darkening like the skies did when clouds rose in them like the time they did when he was in bed, his arms around her, his lips on her.

'A baby… with him?' He stares.

'I am not getting any younger. It needs to happen soon…'

His hands drop off her waist, and he walks away.

'I don't have time, darling,' she moves closer to him. He is thirty-one, and it is odd for her to be with someone younger than her. He said age made no difference, she had to think beyond.

She follows him, and reaches up to kiss him. 'Make love to me,' she whispers. In the flat, they cling together legs, arms, faces, mouths, tongues, thighs, as if one, on the couch, the pile rug, the bed. But afterwards, he raises himself on his elbows and looks at her, 'Do you tell him that as well, to make love to you?'

'Don't start. This is about us.'

'You need to decide Chaya! Now or never?! It's not fair on him, me or even you.'

She scoops her dress from the floor, pulls it over her and leaves.

She is hungry. She walks past the Roast where they have dinner sometimes. The first time, when she ordered a steak, he said, 'I didn't know Indians eat meat.'

'Let's just say I am not a typical Indian!'

'But you grew up there?'

'Yes. But we come in different shapes and sizes! Jokes aside, I am not meant to eat beef. My mother would be horrified.' She had laughed as the blood broke when she cut her rare steak.

'There's so much to know about you. Will I ever?'

That was the first time she had sensed he may want more. The first time she sensed she may want him to want more.

∞

She hurries home now, looking at her phone every couple of minutes. Nothing from Ronan.

The smell of cooking is strong as she walks into the house. They are just getting ready to eat.

'You must be hungry.'

'Yes, I am. Starving.'

Her mother looks surprised, but so happy, that Chaya feels guilty she hasn't been enthusiastic about the extraordinary spread she has been making for the last few days. Now she ladles king prawns cooked in a rich masala of onions and ginger, aubergines fried in circles, white rice, yellow dal, minced lamb with peas on a plate.

'Too much, Ma,' Chaya protests.

'Eat while you can, you won't get this when they leave in

a few days!' Satyan laughs.

'What have you eaten for lunch today?' her mother asks.

'Crayfish and avocado salad. Pret.'

'All this cold food isn't good for you. Nice warm Indian food is what you need.'

'Eat up, eat up,' her father says.

After dinner, he says, 'Have a ladoo.'

'Ma has made ladoos?'

'Yes, for a puja,' Satyan says. 'I had one as well.'

'Why are they... so black?'

'Just a special type. Do you like it?'

'Yes Ma, it's all great. I loved the prawns. Just like when I was younger.'

'It was always your favourite, beti. We all need our childhood food. It completes us. It's our manna.'

She thinks of Ronan alone in his flat having dinner. She texts him goodnight from the bedroom.

∞

She wakes up to the smell of something frying, she hears the oil sputter, Satyan's voice, 'Upma today! Lucky us.'

'A warm breakfast is what you both need. I am making some nice coffee as well, Indian style. None of this cappuccino stuff for Chaya,' she hears her mother say.

She has never liked upma, though her mother makes it well. Black mustard seeds, thin sliced chillies and fragrant coriander leaves in white grains of semolina. She spoons some into her mouth, wanting to knock on the blue door instead, share a flaky croissant from Mable's and remove the crumbs gently from the corner of Ronan's lips. With him she feels she has enough. The baby which doesn't come, pulling at her, haunting her all the time here in the house, disappears. Once she has a baby hands in hers, maybe she will be able to forget Ronan? But what if she never has a baby? Will her life with Satyan ever be enough? She checks her phone, still nothing.

∞

'See, she is eating so much better now. She has to come back to her roots, eat the food she is meant to, and soon she will conceive. Wait and see,' Rukmini tells Prasad. 'They are both looking happier, don't you think? Now let me go outside, do the puja and offer ladoos to the spirits.'

'You think everything is about food and prayers,' sighs Prasad.

'But it is!' she starts to gather ingredients for the puja. On a bronze tray, she arranges a pot of incense sticks, a diya, the bowl of black balls, the little puja bell, and some of the orange flowers from the borders outside.

Halfway to the station, Chaya realises she has forgotten her phone. She rushes back, she's left it on the dining table perhaps. The house feels strangely quiet. Then she notices the conservatory door open, her father outside watching her mother in the garden. She is sitting cross-legged on the grass, smoke curls from some incense sticks, a diya burns with a bright flame. Her mother tries to shield it from the light breeze that flaps at her saree. Her face is rapt, her red bindi, prominent in the greyness. Everything is still. A single autumn leaf flutters down.

Her father sees her, turns, and says, 'Shhh… shhh,' he gestures and walks inside.

'What on earth is she doing?'

'A puja. Don't worry, she means no harm.'

'But why is she sitting there… on the grass?' She can't help but laugh. A gentle tinkling sounds as her mother shakes the puja bell.

'You know her… she always means well,' she sees her father's eyes grow with affection, his smile grow until he also starts laughing.

'I know,' she stands close to him watching her mother.

Then he says, 'You forgot your phone. It's been ringing, quite a few times…'

She returns his smile, picks up the phone, and rushes outside.

Author notes

The Boatboy is a fictionalised account based on the true life story of Baji Raut, from Odisha. The line 'Nuhen bandhu, nuhen, eha chita, e desha timira tale e alibha mukati salita' is from the poem Baji Raut by the Jnanpith award winning Odia poet Sachidananda Routray.

The **Golem of Prague** is a popular folkloric monster involving the mystical Golem of Jewish legend. It is also one of the tales most often told when warning others of the dangers of creating a robot/Golem since they are notoriously hard to control
Robotic process automation (RPA) is the application of technology that allows to configure computer software or a **robot** to capture and interpret existing applications for processing a transaction. Robotic Process Automation is rapidly spreading through enterprises with an objective of reducing costs and increasing efficiencies. A single robot can take over the work of up to six humans. Artificial intelligence in enterprises takes over from robotic process automation and seeks to bring in further efficiencies. In current times, jobs are routinely lost to these technological inventions.

Acknowledgements

This has to start with a big thank you to Farhana Shaikh, inspiring wearer of many hats, for being a beacon for the short story form and forever championing the voice of The Asian Writer. For encouraging me, supporting my writing over the years, and for letting me know one fantastic day, that Dahlia Books would like to publish this collection. These stories had been sitting patiently in my laptop and it is only fitting they find their way in the world through you. Thank you to the whole team at Dahlia Books, including placement students Amelia Haycock and Dhavina Contractor.

Several of these stories have been listed in leading competitions. I would like to thank the judges for the validation these listings provided: The Asian Writer for *Formations* (Winner, 2018) and *The Boatboy* (Shortlist, 2017) Fish Short story for *The Temple Cleaner* (Longlist, 2017), Bath Short Story for *Secrets* (Longlist, 2019) Bristol Short Story for *The Sense of Skin* (Shortlist, 2019), Leicester Writes for *Natural Accents* (Shortlist 2018). A slightly different version of this collection was shortlisted by the SI Leeds Literary Award in 2018; thanks to the judges and the team for that special journey you sent us on, especially Fiona Goh for your skilful coordination, and Irenosen Okojie for your brilliant championing.

Many of these stories have been first read and workshopped by The Whole Kahani, over tea in London. Thank you for the useful feedback and friendship.

My family who have always encouraged my writing journey, especially my mother Mamata Dash, and uncle Jayanarayan Mahapatra for reading many of these stories in earlier drafts. Thank you Krish and Kaustubh for never resenting the time I spend with my stories.

To Selma Carvalho, my writing lifeline; to the readers and friends who have appreciated my work and cheered me on, thank you! This collection would not be here without you all.

About the Author

Mona Dash is the author of A *Roll of the Dice: a story of loss, love and genetics*, winner of Eyelands Book Award 2020 for memoir. Her other published books include two collections of poetry, *A Certain Way* and *Dawn-drops*, and a novel *Untamed Heart*. She has been listed in various competitions, and published widely in various journals and anthologies. She is a member of the British South Asian writers' collective, The Whole Kahani. With a degree in engineering, an MBA, and a Masters in Creative Writing she works in a global tech company. Mona lives in London.

Visit her website: http://www.monadash.net